H.I. TECH

M. Alan Jacobs

ISBN: 1463566395
ISBN 13: 9781463566395
Library of Congress Control Number: 2011909727
CreateSpace, North Charleston, SC

Chapter One

July 19, 1999 was a bad night to be in the observatory. But it was a worse night to be away from the telescope and watching the observatory television. Raymond Marsden was on CNN predicting the end of the world.

Not that H.I. Tech gave a damn about the news, and not that he was the kind of sixteen-year-old geek who watched CNN. H.I. Tech knew he was definitely a geek, but not that kind. He simply knew his place in the world and didn't like it. His build was tall, but it was all arms and legs. His face was all wrong for his age, already lean and angular and dark. And he had to shave every day. Shaving should have been a good thing, because it made him look older. But looking older was a good thing only if it went along with being cool. And he was damn sure he sucked at being cool. He wasn't even cool enough to go against Doc's rules and cold-boot the chip inside the cable box to get an honest-to-God entertainment channel. Cold-booting and reprogramming the decoder would have been a snap for him. But instead he marched to Doc's orders. To make himself feel better, he told himself that even the toughest S.O.B. in school would have done the same as him growing up with Doc as a father.

The observatory was built out of what had once been an empty attic and had been given as a fifteenth birthday present. It had come complete with big skylights and a telescope engraved with the name H.I. Tech. H.I. still thanked God it was only his initials on the scope. He hated his name. That sort of made him even with Doc, who didn't like being called Dad. So H.I.'s sixteenth birthday had come with a privilege instead of a gift. From that point forward he was to call his father "Doc". It was supposed to be more grown-up that way, man to man. On the same birthday, Doc had also tried to make his case that astronomy was an easy beginner science. He'd hoped H.I. would spend more time in the observatory. H. I. did spend more time. But not doing what Doc had wanted! Not in the least.

For starters, Doc had been deliberately misleading about astronomy. Nice try on Doc's part, but no way was Doc going to get him to fall for any reverse psychology trick. No way was astronomy easy or for beginners. It was not just about looking through a scope and cataloguing distant objects. Astronomy was about complex physics and advanced math. And astronomers were members of a pretty rough club. They got in lots of fights with each other and with zealots. Always had and maybe always would. For sure, they were fight magnets. Not a crowd or a hobby that looked good to H.I. Tech. He already had enough bullshit in his life.

H.I. did spend some time looking through his scope. But not at the sky. Not until a July night when he realized that what he liked to watch on the scope was really gone and never coming back. It was the same night that Raymond Marsden told Larry King that the world was about to end.

It was hot outside the Beltway that night, just as hot as it was in DC. There was no air-conditioning in the observatory, just a ceiling fan that stirred stale summer air as if it were soup. So H.I. stripped to his undershirt and boxers, opened the north skylight, and cursed the neighbors who'd finished building a third-floor playroom between Doc's house and April Waterstone's. H.I. used to aim his telescope at her window four blocks away, feel good just catching her silhouette against the curtains or catching a glimpse of blonde hair if the curtains were cracked. She was the only reason he ever spent time in the observatory. And even after the playroom hid her window, he'd point the scope anyway. He'd find her roof and listen to music.

That night he didn't listen to music, didn't want to hear some rocker with more girlfriends than he could count sing about lost love. So he followed Doc's rules, turned on CNN and watched Larry King introduce Marsden as a professor of astronomy from Yale. Marsden was not supposed to be King's guest that night. In fact King pre-empted his scheduled program to make room for him, announcing that Marsden was about to reveal something startling on the eve of the 30th anniversary of mankind's first walk on the moon. A true scientist, King called Marsden. But H.I.'d seen scientists before. He'd grown up with Doc and knew what a true scientist looked like. Marsden didn't fit. He seemed scared, damn scared. But not about being on TV.

"So what you're telling this audience, Dr. Marsden, is that this finding was purely accidental." King's voice was more raspy than usual. He buried his chin in his hand, almost looked bored. Marsden didn't look bored.

"I prefer to call it unexpected." Marsden blinked and tried to straighten his wiry, blond and gray hair. He played nervously with his glasses. Some might have thought he wasn't used to the lights of a television studio. Or they might have thought he felt trapped by the tiny collar microphone that kept him leashed to his chair. The maybes would have been wrong, but H.I. wouldn't have been among them. H.I. knew immediately that what scared Marsden was the knowledge he was about to disclose.

"At first I thought this was a sporadic, but…"

"A sporadic, Doctor Marsden? Can you explain this to our audience?"

"Yes, a sporadic. A non-shower meteor. Shower meteors occur on a predictable basis, as the Earth passes through known storms. They are seasonal. In contrast, sporadics are unknowns, usually the debris of an extinct comet dispersed over the dead comet's orbit. They are the skeletal remains of a dead comet, if you will. They come out of nowhere."

CNN did a close up on Marsden's first astro-photograph, a time-exposed picture taken using a telescope as the camera lens. Marsden's voice cracked. "What you are seeing on this first plate should not be there."

The photograph was just a faint white line slashed across a field of distant stars, sort of like the barest of chalk marks on an old blackboard. Still, this faint, bare streak was brighter than the background star field. Explaining it, Marsden forced strength into his voice.

"Ordinarily a streak like this one, appearing on time-lapse, would indicate something moved across the field. Something that reflected the sun's light back into the camera lens. Ordinarily one would assume an asteroid or a meteorite."

Marsden blinked a lot, and he was sweating. H.I. knew that the studio wasn't like his damn observatory. It had to be air-conditioned in that studio, but Marsden was sweating like it wasn't. King's efforts to put him at ease were failing big time. Raymond Marsden spoke as if he knew no one would believe what he was about to say. He spoke like a man afraid of his own warning.

"This streak should not be here in this part of the night sky. And at this distance, only an object with huge mass could reflect this kind of light. But an object of such large mass would not have had such velocity."

"You said this was an accidental finding?" King shrugged.

"Yes. It was captured during a teaching exercise. That's why I also have this spectrograph."

The spectrograph wasn't much to see, either, just a plate of colors separated into dozens of horizontal lines. Marsden explained that the technique involved focusing light from his meteor or asteroid through a prism, separating the light into a band of colors, and matching it with his computer. Every element in the universe would give off a certain band, sort of like a fingerprint. His meteor or asteroid had not followed the rules. It couldn't be matched with anything. H.I. Tech told himself he was beginning to like that meteor.

"Dr. Marsden, are you telling this television audience that you have discovered something unknown to science?"

"That's exactly what I am saying." Marsden wiped his glasses.

"So your equipment is unable to identify any part of this sporadic, as you call it?"

"I can identify part."

"Which part is that, Doctor?" King spoke as if he were reading cue cards prepared by Marsden himself, sort of building a case answer by answer. H.I. knew that Marsden would have to live with the consequences, but King would not.

"The spectrograph shows the meteorite is trailing a cloud of radioactive ions."

"Is this a natural phenomenon, like, say, a comet?" King had done his homework.

"No. A comet is basically a dirty snowball. It trails an alphabet soup of ionized gas and vapor. This spectrograph shows only one kind of ion, hydrogen. This signature is similar to what I would expect from an ion drive engine, the kind now undergoing tests in Nevada."

"Are you saying this sporadic is man-made?"

"No. It is too distant in space."

"Are you saying it is being driven by some sort of engine?"

"It's possible."

"Are you calling it a UFO?"

"Accepting that *UFO* merely means unidentified, I would have to say yes."

Watching Marsden, H.I. felt sorry for him. At least, he sort of felt sorry for him. Marsden wasn't the only scientist he'd seen slit his own throat on TV. Not literally, of course. But he remembered the guys who'd claimed they could produce cold fusion in a bottle in their lab. If those guys were real lucky, no one else on the planet would remember them. Not even their own families. And if those guys were super lucky, no one would remember cold fusion, either, because they'd been way off the reservation when they'd thought it up. There was no such thing as cold fusion and never would be. Not that the news agencies who'd carried their story had known the difference between cold fusion and cold pizza. The news agencies had just been interested in filler material on a slow news day. The point was if these guys had ever even had university positions, they'd flushed them down the toilet the second they'd stepped in front of the camera. And if they were employed these days, they were probably teaching high school somewhere and glad to get a paycheck. So watching Marsden, H.I. figured he'd probably just kissed his Yale position good-bye.

After a break for a commercial, King returned with his scheduled program, part two of an interview with Madonna. H.I. turned off the TV, went back to his telescope, and told himself the only heavenly body on his sky chart was still April Waterstone. But what he wanted to see wasn't there. The fricking neighbors' playroom was still in his way. It always would be. He lay on the matted window seat and used his imagination. But he didn't last long.

He fell asleep looking at the sky. Falling asleep in the observatory was always a bad idea. After Marsden's interview, it was a very bad idea. He dreamed about night, not a night filled with stars, but the black kind filled with dread that goes all the way into your stomach. It was endless and deep. There were no stars at all. There never would be.

He woke falling and soaked in sweat, still on the window seat. He woke with Marsden's problem in his head. It was six a.m., and he was late for work.

Twenty minutes later, H.I. Tech was rolling newspapers at the Waterstone house. He always began his route there, gave himself an excuse to hang out where he wasn't invited. The morning after Marsden's CNN appearance, he skimmed the last copy of the *Washington Post* before he rolled it. Marsden was in the first section, on a back page. His story followed a slightly larger one celebrating the 30th anniversary of Neil Armstrong's first step on the moon in 1969 and asking about the future of NASA. Marsden was in the spotlight. Poor fricking, scared Raymond Marsden.

The *Post* reported that he needed three additional astrophotographs to calculate the orbit of his meteor. He didn't have them. Colleagues called him irresponsible and incompetent. They said he'd probably observed a meteor trail in Earth's atmosphere and confused it with a distant object. As for his spectrograph, it wasn't calibrated properly, or maybe he had a glitch in his software.

H.I. rolled the *Post,* slipped it back into its plastic bag, dropped it at the porch, and was halfway to the street when he heard the front door open and slam shut. He turned, like he did every morning and watched Dr. Kay Waterstone cross the yard to climb into her Suburban. He waited for her at the street, like he did every morning. "Dr. Kay" was what he called her. That was her idea. She told kids that she liked to call her Dr. Kay instead of Dr. Waterstone.

Driver's window down, she stopped her Suburban at the edge of the driveway, swept black hair from her face, and studied H.I. from head to foot. Her eyes caught his attention, always did. They were deep and liquid blue like April's. And just like April, she made little creases under them when she smiled.

"Hey, handsome." Her voice was throaty. H.I. loved it.

"You talking to me?"

"I said 'handsome,' didn't I?" She had the same face as April, high cheekbones, round mouth, and delicate chin.

The two also shared the same build, tall with slender curves. But Dr. Kay was as olive and dark haired as her Italian mother while April's looks came from her father, gilded skin and hair like wheat. H.I knew the story about April's father. He was blown up by a terrorist bomb in a marine barracks in the Middle East before she was born. H.I. used to tell himself that not knowing her father was why April was moody. But H.I. knew better, and as far as he could tell, so did Dr. Kay.

" Anyone ever say you work too hard?" she asked.

"Not anyone in my house."

"How many jobs you working these days?"

"As many as it takes."

"To do what?"

"To support your daughter in the style to which she's accustomed. I plan to make her happy."

"April? Happy?" She looked at him intently, "Anyone ever tell you that making April happy is impossible?"

"It wouldn't matter. I'm not the negative type."

"Smitten aren't you, handsome?" She rolled up the window and pulled away. At the street, she braked and waved, following the same routine as every morning. But that morning would be the last.

An hour and a half later, H.I. Tech was sacking at Dunbar's Grocery and staring at Marsden's photo on the front page of every tabloid in the rack. Marsden shared space with his astro-photograph and black-and-white drawings of flying saucers and little aliens. H.I. felt sorry for Marsden. He really did. Like him, H.I. was reaching for something he could never have.

"She ain't comin' this early, man." Jefferson Parrish was suddenly beside H.I. and ready to catch him watching the soda fountain in Dunbar's annex. Jefferson knew H.I. didn't give a damn about milkshakes. He knew H.I. cared about who sat there with her girlfriends most afternoons. Jefferson Parrish was the only black kid at school and the only black checker in Dunbar's. He mostly stuck to himself. H.I. liked to think that they had that much in common, both of them being one-of-a-kind. Maybe that was why Jefferson understood him.

"What *she* are you talking about?" H.I. tried to look confused. But he wasn't a good actor, either.

"I'm talkin' about your girlfriend, man." Jefferson grinned. "April ain't comin' this early. She never gets here before four. She may not get here at all, man."

"I still don't know what you're talking about."

"Tech, you are one lousy bullshit artist, baby."

Jefferson shrugged him off. Four p.m. came and went, and the soda fountain seats stayed empty. Outside, it looked like rain. H.I. blamed April's absence on the weather. By five p.m., a new set of tabloids reached the rack. Marsden made the covers of three, having claimed to have his additional photo plates and a preliminary fix on his meteor. In typical fashion, he'd named his meteor for the year of its discovery and his initials. RM 1999. The story shared space with a psychic who predicted the end of the world.

By nine p.m., H.I. was back in the observatory, and Marsden was back on CNN facing Larry King. The lights in the observatory were off, and the south skylight was open. The heat and lights of DC bounced back from low rain clouds. The sky was a brilliant shade of wet gray.

"You're aware, Dr. Marsden, that none of your colleagues has duplicated or confirmed your findings?" King said.

"Well aware. They looked in the wrong part of the sky. RM 1999 has behaved in a very unexpected, even unlikely manner."

The camera did a close-up on a series of new astro-photographs. Marsden spoke with more confidence than his first appearance on Larry King. H.I. told himself that maybe Marsden was feeling that he had backup. But confidence and backup aside, Marsden still looked scared shit-less, like a green soldier going into combat for the first time in an old WWII movie on late night TV. Or so Jefferson had described the look, since technically H.I. wasn't supposed to have fricking entertainment channels.

"All these additional plates were made by amateurs, one in New Mexico, one in Arizona, and one in California. Judging by these observations, I'd estimate that RM 1999 is traveling at great speed."

The amateur from Tucson had made a calculated guess at RM 1999's speed. He'd slowed the driving clock of his time-lapse accordingly, and his astro-photograph showed the stars as elongate streaks and RM 1999 frozen in space. It wasn't much to see, just a faint, distant white dot.

Marsden seemed to steel himself before speaking again. "In my estimation, RM 1999 will impact the Earth within forty-eight hours. It will strike the atmosphere at a speed of one hundred and sixty thousand miles per hour, the same speed as the meteor that destroyed the dinosaurs and changed the direction of life on Earth as we know it. RM 1999 will do the same to humankind."

King broke for a commercial.

When he returned, he and Marsden were joined by a panel of experts, mostly university types but one from

NASA and another from the Space Command branch of the Air Force. From Marsden's standpoint, it had to be Custer's last stand. The panel spent the next hour tearing apart everything that Marsden had to say. Marsden's find was just another NEO, a Near-Earth Object. It was already under study, not even a fraction as big or fast as Marsden had said. It posed no threat.

H.I. turned off the TV and slept in his room. Sleep was dreamless.

The morning *Post* mentioned nothing about Marsden or RM 1999. H.I. read it before he went to the Waterstone's. He got there late, late enough to find a gray sedan with government plates backing away from Dr. Kay's Suburban. The driver was black and maybe mid-thirties. He kept his face out of sight, smoked a cigarette, and seemed to avoid looking at his passenger. The sedan backed into the street, and H.I. caught a glimpse of Dr. Kay in the passenger seat. There was no doubt in his mind that it was her. And there was no doubt that she seemed upset. H.I. didn't like it, seeing Dr. Kay upset. He fixed his eyes on her, but she didn't look in his direction as the gray sedan moved away slowly and headed out of sight toward the Beltway.

Once the car was gone, H.I. headed toward the house. All of the lights were out. The note on the front door was in Dr. Kay's handwriting.

Handsome,

April left town yesterday. I'm gone today. See you end of the summer. Don't drop off any newspapers. Dottie will take care of the mail. Stop working so hard.

Love, Dr. Kay.

H.I. scanned the whole front of the Waterstone house. He looked at the dark windows, got seriously pissed off, and threw the papers over the fence. He checked on it every day the rest of the summer, but it stayed dark.

Forty-eight hours after Marsden's prediction, RM 1999 impacted the atmosphere over the mid-Atlantic. Radio-active ions spewing along its mile-long tail set off alarms throughout NORAD and its counterpart in Russia. The fire-ball created a three-hundred-mile-per-hour windstorm and traversed the Atlantic in eight minutes. The eight-minute fireball and its tail were visible on four continents.

Most news agencies later praised the high-level com-mand decisions that prevented panic in both the U.S. and Russia, which may have led to misinterpretation and nu-clear missile launches. Independent reporters asked how the generals on both sides managed to keep their cool. The tabloids on the stand at Dunbar's implied a conspiracy. Some even implied that the firestorms were man-made, the result of nukes launched from east and west in an attempt to destroy RM 1999. Marsden himself was not available for comment. None of the news agencies seemed to notice his absence. H.I. did.

The last report was a brief flash on CNN stating that RM 1999 had impacted harmlessly in a far corner of the Ama-zon rain forest. One of the correspondents held a micro-phone in the smiling face of one of the same experts who had disputed Marsden forty-eight hours earlier. The expert concluded that RM 1999 was a small comet. He said it was of no importance.

By the first day of school, April was back, and H.I. was dropping the *Post* in front of her house. He glimpsed a flash of long blonde hair in the windows. Dr. Kay was nowhere in sight. The Suburban was collecting soot in the driveway. Dottie Sinclair answered the door when H.I. knocked.

"Where's Dr. Kay?"

"Out of the country on sabbatical," Dottie answered through the crack. She always watched April when Dr. Kay was out of town. Dottie was young, but looked even younger, could have passed for a high-school kid. She treated April like a sister. April liked that part. When Dottie's husband was out of town, which was a lot, she kept a very loose rein on April Waterstone. April liked that part too.

"Know when she'll be back?"

"I can't say. You know these scientists." Dottie narrowed the crack so that only half of her face was visible.

"Unfortunately I do."

"Dottie!" April's voice came from another room, throaty like Dr. Kay but much louder and harsher. She had to know he was there, H.I. told himself. But she stayed out of sight and shouted louder, "Dottie! Coffee!"

Dottie smiled sympathetically and closed the door without inviting him in. It was the same routine every morning. Same questions but no real answers. By Fall, RM 1999 and Marsden were forgotten, somehow even by the tabloids. Like the expert who'd dismissed Marsden, the tabloids decided RM 1999 was of no importance, that it was an ex-event. H.I. forgot about it too. But of course none of them were in the Amazon when it came down.

Chapter Two

The upper Amazon basin. The Jivanos Indians reached it just before the great fire fell from the sky.

The shaman led them up the smaller river to it, far away from the great river and the cloth-covered people whose great shiny beasts ate the forest and the earth. He led them toward where the water began. There he promised them they would see the last horizon, where the forest met mountains so wise they were capped in white. It was the edge of the world, the place where the sun slept. The shaman told them they would live as one with the Earth, waiting for the end that would come when the sun fell in a rain of fire from the night sky.

And so they watched the great fire descend in a summer sky more angry than the sky had ever been. The Earth shook and roared upward, hiding the sky in a great dark smoke that turned day into night. The light bore deep into the Earth, and where it rested, the forest animals and birds filled the darkness with their screams. The terror and the screaming lasted for days, numbered only by the times sleep took the Jivanos away. When the smoke cleared, a great hole lay where the forest had been, and a new sun had taken the old one's place in the sky. The Shaman went to see what had happened to the old one. He never returned.

The Jivanos waited.

Five months later, Dr. Kay watched them. She stood at the perimeter of the cyclone fence, hugged herself in her lab coat, and watched them gathered in their communal hut. She watched them every morning and decided they were afraid. She understood why.

"You look cold, Dr. Waterstone." Major Smith was suddenly standing next to her, handing her coffee.

Dr. Kay took the steel thermos in both hands. Mornings carried a chill. The Marine coffee warmed her fingers and it tasted good. It wasn't supposed to do either.

"Thanks." Dr. Kay told herself she felt safe with Smith. The green fatigues, the soft cap, and the aviator glasses reminded of her of the man she'd lost a lifetime before. They'd both been so young. She'd still been in school, pregnant with April when April's father had died.

"Why do I rate your company this morning?" Dr. Kay took another sip.

"Saw you looked cold."

She tried to laugh. It came out weak. She looked at Smith. Behind the aviator glasses, she sensed an intense stare, but little warmth. The rest of his narrow face was pale, expressionless, almost mask-like. She knew the type, always on the job and covering every conceivable loose end.

"Actually, the com link's down." Smith held up his radio. It emitted a harsh sound. "Nothing but static. Can't raise my patrols. Your boys swear it's not EMI." Smith referred to electromagnetic interference. His patrols were supposed to walk the edges of the impact crater and keep the Jivanos at a safe distance. Dr. Kay knew Smith was going by the manual, keeping the Jivanos away. It was unnecessary. The Jivanos were not going anywhere near the crater. They'd dropped their bows and blowguns and stayed huddled together in their communal hut. They kept their women and children sheltered in the center. They accepted food and water from the American marines. Otherwise, they did not move.

Dr. Kay turned and looked across brown faces and bowl cut heads of black hair. The Jivanos did not look back. They were waiting.

"Anyway, I thought I'd check things out myself." Smith didn't smile. His face was a frozen mask. "Relax, Doctor Waterstone. You worry too much."

"I'm not worried. I'm scared to death." Dr. Kay turned and walked back into the compound. She sensed Smith watching her. She reminded herself she felt safe with him.

Twenty yards from the fence, she entered the first rows of tents where a platoon of marines, forty-two officers and men, was bivouacked. Major Smith was the company commander. One American platoon was all that the Brazilian government had allowed into the country. The rest of his company was still at sea. A Brazilian guard occupied the inner row of tents, sent to overlook the Americans. The two units did not mix. None of the marines spoke Portuguese.

Crossing the inner row, Dr. Kay felt eyes on her. She turned and saw the Brazilian commanding officer. Clad in a highly decorated uniform, he flashed a smile at her. He had brilliant white teeth. She nodded back.

Inside the second row, she stepped around a microwave dish and looked into the communications tent. Two marine communications specialists were seated at the equipment. One of them noticed her.

"Satellite link-up is in twenty minutes, Doc. We need five to code." The technician held up his watch.

Dr. Kay nodded and pointed to her own watch. She started to walk away. Then she turned back. "Your signal check out okay?"

"In the green, Doc."

"Any interference this morning?"

"No. Should there be?"

She walked away without answering. She walked fast, heading toward the concrete and steel control complex.

The construction had been completed in less than two weeks. The facility had become operational less than six weeks after RM 1999 had fallen from the sky. By then, RM 1999 had been given a new designation known only in secure circles. She knew it wouldn't stay secure. Somehow there always seemed to be leaks. Unlike what was reported by the press, RM 1999 had come down quite intact. It was now designated Object Alpha Bell Tower.

Bell Tower! The name wasn't her idea. Actually, it gave her the creeps. She shivered every time she thought of it. So would any sane person.

In fact, she hadn't been the only one to get the creeps. But she had been the only one to think things through and suggest how to get self-contained technology on site in the Amazon. The military types had listened to her. Maybe because she knew how to talk with them. Came with the territory, she would always tell herself. Came from having been married to a marine.

The on-site technology had existed even before Bell Tower's arrival. They'd existed in the form of materials originally designed for launch into orbit where they were to become part of the international space station. She'd suggested they be borrowed.

The airtight modules had easily been fitted into the cargo hold of the *U.S.S. Harper's Ferry,* a seagoing, seventeen-thousand-ton Navy Landing Ship Dock. *Harper's Ferry* had entered the Amazon at Belem and traveled alone one hundred miles upriver to a full seaport at Manaus. Sikorsky Super-Stallion helicopters had done the rest of the job, airlifting the modules and heavy parts from *Harper's Ferry* to the site of Object Alpha Bell Tower's impact. Afterward the *Harper's Ferry* had joined the helicopter assault ship *U.S.S. Wasp,* the carrier *Nimitz,* and their support group in international waters.

The modules were arrayed in trains and supported on giant cement and steel piers. There was only one working entrance, a single airlock at the top of metal stairs fitted to the aft section of a forty-three foot module built by the Russians. The Russian's construct had been designed to serve and control the international space station. The irony was that the module's builders would not have the security clearance to know that their creation was currently parked in a remote section of the Amazon rain forest under the guard of American marines.

Dr. Kay climbed the grated metal stairs to the small platform that interfaced the service module. Beside the airlock she punched her code into the key pad. The entry light changed from red to green. She cranked open the hatch and felt negatively pressurized air hiss inside as the chamber equalized. She climbed into the airlock and repeated the process with the inner door. The air inside the module stung her nostrils with the acrid stench of human sweat, burned coffee, and old cigarettes. TV monitors, rows of desktop computers, and hastily built electronics covered the length of one bulkhead. Beyond them, everything was naked steel, exposed conduits, and colored wires.

Dr. Kay stared at the back of the one man on duty, Jennings, who like herself was a civilian consultant to ETRAC, Extra-Terrestrial Response and Containment. ETRAC's civilian assets, like Jennings and herself, were never kept completely inside the loop. There were always secrets kept from them, and security was always the excuse that was given. "Level of clearance" was practically a status symbol. The distinction made for friction and distrust. Jennings was loaded with both. She tapped his shoulder, and he turned from a table littered in ashtrays, coffee cups, and laptops.

Jennings finished a Twinkie, licked his fingers, and wiped his hands on filthy jeans and an even filthier T-shirt. To Dr. Kay, he looked like a wannabe middle-aged hippie. Give him a point for appearance, the shaggy hair, chin stubble, and mismatched clothing, she told herself. But then she'd have to take away four points for attitude. Way too much love, peace, and happiness and not near enough tear-down-the-barricades. And both attitudes were in the wrong decade and wrong place for ETRAC. Jennings made no bones about the fact that he expected any extraterrestrial presence to be friendly right up until there was contact with his own superiors, especially those in uniform.

"How's Rambo this morning?" Jennings turned back to his equipment.

"If you mean Colonel Smith, he's acting tough." Dr. Kay shivered. "The colonel says I worry too much."

"No shit, you worry too much. And Rambo's just playing a part. I bet underneath his little combat fatigues, he's just as scared as you are."

"Give it a rest, Jennings." She looked beyond him toward the far hatch that opened to Node One. A light indicated it was locked. Node One was a spherical, steel compartment that connected the service module to the rest of the complex. Beyond Node One, the safe lab module interfaced with Node Two, which acted as a barrier against the isolation area. Beyond isolation was the dreaded Node Three. Isolation and Node Three were closest to the impact crater. The service module, where control was maintained, was the furthest. In an emergency, control would be the place of last defense. But defense against what, Dr. Kay wasn't sure. She turned toward Jennings.

"You pick up any electromagnetic interference this morning?" she asked. "Any spikes at all?"

"No."

"Smith has. Says his hand radios are down."

"It's not coming from the crater." Jennings lit a cigarette. "I've been here since before daybreak. It's been quiet."

"Doesn't make any sense. Why would his hand radios be down?"

"Government issue equipment. Low bid."

Dr. Kay seated herself at the main console and studied the monitors. The feeds all came from cameras aimed into the impact crater. They relayed only fog, freezing fog in the middle of the Amazon. Hidden inside was an impact crater that was wedge-shaped and a mile long. At its west end, the crater's bottom was two hundred feet below the jungle floor. The fog was dense and impenetrable. A radio-linked probe showed a constant ground temperature of -78.5 centigrade. Even though it was nearing the end of the dry season, the Amazon rains should already have turned the crater into a lake. That had not happened. The reason was unknown. What the cameras could find of the crater walls and floor showed them to be as lifeless as the surface of the moon. Prior to impact, the same ground had been rain forest, teeming with life. All animal and plant life had died within hours to days of the impact. RM 1999, now designated Object Alpha Bell Tower, was somewhere in a shrouded abyss of its own making where it was hidden from the cameras, hidden from spectroscopy, unresponsive to radio waves, unresponsive to microwaves, and unresponsive to pulsed sound. The radiation levels were normal background level.

The cause of death for animal life was unknown. The cause of death for plant life was unknown. Object Alpha Bell Tower was a scientific and mathematical X.

Dr. Kay's orders specified that she "identify and quantify the X" . Those orders came from some office deep within the Pentagon. She was not privy to which office, only that the Department of Defense had passed them to her via ETRAC. Her mission was specific.

SUBJECT: ALPHA BELL TOWER page 125 of 324
CLASSIFICATION: TOP SECRET
AUTHORITY: DOD
DEPT: ETRAC
EYES ONLY: K. WATERSTONE (clearance level high security)
MISSION DIRECTIVES:

1. Team leader is to determine whether Object Alpha Bell Tower is a natural phenomenon such as a meteorite or comet. Team leader is to determine the origin of designated object and determine the risk of recurrence.
2. Team leader is to focus investigative efforts toward the isolation of the cause or causes of the deaths that surround the site now designated Crash Site Alpha Bell Tower. Team leader is proceed with such investigations as are needed to determine or to exclude the presence of ionizing radiation, heat, toxic gasses, toxic liquids, toxic vapors, microbial agents or dangerous elements heretofore unidentified.
3. Team leader is to determine whether the element or elements identified in directive 2 represent a clear and present danger beyond the site designated Crash Site Alpha Bell Tower.

Her orders played in her mind a hundred times a day. So did Directive 4, her mission priority.

TEAM LEADER'S FIRST PRIORITY IS CONTAINMENT.

The knowledge of that priority haunted her—what she would have to do if worse came to worse, if containment failed. The order terrified her. That she might fail to carry out the order terrified her even more.

SUBJECT: MISSION OVERRIDE
INITIATOR: FAILURE OF CONTAINMENT
ACTION: RELAY RECOMENDATION FOR OPTION MOP UP AND FOLLOW PROCEDURE AS SPECIFIED IN APPENDIX 1A

Mop Up! The thought sent fear deep into the pit of her. It was the ultimate way to secure Crash Site Alpha Bell Tower. It wasn't a job suited for a scientist. Scientists were suited for measuring, analyzing, and publishing, but history often pulled scientists into doing what they'd never intended. Scientists were supposed to remain objective. *They* were not supposed to consider their personal feelings. Anything personal created bias, and bias was the enemy of science. But it was impossible to avoid what was personal.

Dr. Kay thought of April every minute, agonized over what would happen to April and everyone else if she did her job wrong. An inner voice told Dr. Kay that she was not suited for the decision she might have to make.

Major Smith was better suited, she told herself. He was military, and he was supposed to understand weapons, be prepared to use them. He understood defense. He'd said there were people in the world who would just love to take Object Alpha Bell Tower apart and use it for a weapon.

Smith had said that he had limited resources to deal with threats to the security of Crash Site Alpha Bell Tower and that time was working against him. She'd promised him the progress would be swift. So far no progress had been made. And there had been human deaths, four of her own team members. Her reports summed up her failure.

TO: DEPARTMENT OF DEFENSE
EYES ONLY: J. RAMSEY (clearance level high security)
BRIEFING OFFICER: J. RAMSEY
FROM: K. WATERSTONE
DIRECTIVE: ETRAC
CLASSIFICATION: TOP SECRET
SUBJECT: ALPHA BELL TOWER
MISSION STATUS: Loss of life is from cause unknown. Level of threat beyond Crash Site Alpha Bell Tower is unknown. Containment status is assumed and not confirmed.Indentity of Bell Tower Object is unkown.

A failed effort! It had been so from the very start, based on the erroneous presumption that tools developed by Earth science could be used to study something of non-Earth origin. There was still the possibility that X-rays or ultrasound could penetrate Alpha Bell Tower to yield information. But the equipment would have to be carried to Crash Site Alpha Bell Tower by humans. That had already been tried once, and four of her colleagues had died in the process. Died horribly. She blamed herself. They'd gone into the crater on her orders.

Dr. Kay turned to the infrared and radar monitors. The radar image was a blip, a half-sphere the size of a warehouse. It was completely still and lifeless in the bottom of the crater. The radar image never changed. The infrared image was different. It looked alive.

"Boo." Jennings laughed and watched Dr. Kay cringe. "Jeez, Waterstone. You'd think it was going to bite you."

"Four of your coworkers are dead, Jennings. Think about that."

She fixed her gaze on the infrared image, fed to her monitor via a computer from Landsat sensors placed at the crater edge. The sensors received near-visible infrared light reflected from their target,broke the light into spectral bands, and the let the computer assign each band a color based on the whim of the operator. Jennings was the operator. He assigned the object its color.

The giant yellow orb was motionless in the center of the screen, surrounded in streams of gray. It was waiting. It was looking at her. She felt it. She said so.

"You have too much imagination for this job, Waterstone." She ignored him.

"Personally, I think you've got something against yellow. Not me. My first V.W. Beetle was yellow."

She didn't respond.

"It's not like the damn thing is alive!" Jennings stubbed out his cigarette, leaned back in his chair, and laughed. "Sometimes I think you're actually worse than Smith."

She thought of Major Smith and the malfunctioning hand radios. She gave Jennings instructions. "Change the inclination angle on your infrareds. Set your differentials to ID people. Sweep the crater rim, 200 to 160."

"Expecting dinner guests?"

"I want to know where Smith's people are."

Jennings did what he was told. The sweep showed nothing. Neither did a sweep with the sound sensors.

"Where the hell are those marine patrols?"

Jennings didn't answer. He realigned his sensors into the crater. He froze. She saw the look on his face. "What's the matter?"

"I saw movement."

"What are you talking about?"

"Movement. Surface oscillations—soon as I realigned the sensor. Bell Tower's skin, surface, whatever you want to call it. It moved."

"Don't play with me, Jennings."

"I'm not. I promise on my Berkley diploma."

"You didn't go to Berkley."

She turned to face the infrared monitor and forgot all about sparing with Jennings. The screen was gray, nothing but swirling gray. The object was gone.

"Oh, my God." She reached for the nearest keyboard.

Jennings's eyes were already on infrared screen. He began sweating and flicked his eyes to the radar. "It's not gone." He relaxed. "Radar still shows a blip."

Just as suddenly, the radar blip winked off. Ten seconds later, it was back, unchanged, visible for less than a second each time the sweep passed. In the same instant, the yellow orb returned on infrared. It was motionless. Dr. Kay could feel it waiting.

"I'm calling Smith." She picked up her hand radio, but got only static. She turned to Jennings. "Level one alert. All department chiefs to control now!"

At that moment, Major Flap Smith was walking the cyclone fence perimeter, as he did every morning. For the fifth time, he raised his short-range hand-held radio and transmitted his call. For the fifth time, his answer was static.

Static meant things were going according to his plan. His plan and not the one handed down in his orders.

Smith considered his orders. They called for the impossible. That was usual for marines. And most of the time, marines got the impossible done. But this time they wouldn't. Because on site, he was in charge. Because he had his own plans, and those plans had nothing to do with official marine orders.

They'd given him one Sapper platoon, a unit of combat engineers. The Brazilian government had allowed it only because of the engineer designation. He had assumed command of the platoon at sea. His mission classification was Marine Expeditionary Unit—Special Operations Capable—designation TRAP. The last part stood for Tactical Recovery of Aircraft and Personnel. Only he knew he wasn't

recovering aircraft or personnel. He wasn't supposed to
know.

They hadn't told him exactly what was in the crater, only
that in the wrong hands it could be made into a weapon.
His orders and his briefing had been focused on a narrow
mission.

SECURE THE PERIMETER FROM PERSON OR PERSONS UNKNOWN.

Smith knew the protocol: keep three fire teams patrol-
ling the crater rim at all times. Each fire team consisted of a
corporal equipped with an M16 and grenade launcher, two
riflemen equipped with M16s, and one automatic rifleman
equipped with a squad automatic weapon. Considerable
fire power when the weapons were loaded. But modifica-
tions in his orders had specified that the weapons not be
loaded. That modification had come courtesy of Pentagon
lawyers concerned about accidental shooting in a friendly
country. That was bad for the marines under his command,
but good for his personal plan.

Each of the three teams was under the command of a
sergeant. That left the rest of his platoon, its remaining six
fire teams and sergeants, their staff sergeant, and first lieutenant, in the bivouac. Two of the men would be in the
communications tent at all times. All in all, it was a small
force with which to do his job.

A small force was perfect, but not for carrying out the
official orders.

He wondered only briefly, what would the real Major
Flap Smith do? It was a mute question. The real Major Flap
Smith wasn't here. He was anchored in concrete and feed-

ing the fish hundreds of feet down and three miles off the Virginia coast.

Smith looked beyond the cyclone fence at the Jivanos. Their eyes looked east toward the jungle, but he knew their collective conscious was focused in the direction of the crater. Maybe they sensed something there. The Jivanos were hunters, lived off of the land, knew how to make weapons from the trees and stones, how to use plants to poison the tip of their darts and arrows. They knew the importance of stealth.

Smith saw it in their faces. They felt the presence of another hunter.

Maybe they felt the vibrations in the Earth or smelled something in the wind. Maybe they just knew. He considered the irony of it. Savages could sense something a combat hardened soldier could not.

He tried a last time to raise his patrols. Nothing but static. That was according to plan. He dropped his radio.

Smith walked to the north fence and stood in plain view of the low jungle hills. He lit a cigar, as he did every morning. This time, he dropped it without taking more than a puff. He let it burn where it fell and walked back into camp. His first lieutenant and staff sergeant were in his command tent when he found them.

"Dress inspection in two minutes. Assemble your squads."

"Sir?"

"You heard me. Inspection! We've got Brazilian VIPs en route. Look like engineers. No arms."

"No visits are on the schedule."

"Just came in on the radio. Make ready."

"Aye, aye, sir."

Smith walked to the communications tent and found two of his technicians bent over their equipment. They saluted and went back to work, their backs toward him. Smith removed the silenced .22 magnum automatic from his jacket and did his job at close range with two muffled shots no louder than a cap pistol's. Then he left, closing the tent flap behind him. He knew the tent would not be disturbed.

In the service module, Dr. Kay faced her coworkers. She checked her watch, took a last look at the monitors, and made her pronouncement. "I've called level one because five minutes ago Bell Tower went off the scope."

"What do you mean it went off the scope?"

"She means radar and infrared could no longer see it," Jennings answered before Dr. Kay could. "For ten seconds we couldn't prove it was still in the crater." He wandered to the steel wall and looked out of a porthole.

The shouting came from all directions, all at once.

"Must have been a hardware glitch."

"Did you check the BUS?"

"Radar and infrared are on a separate BUS, fed from opposite ends of the complex."

"You guys aren't listening," Jennings interrupted. "There was nothing wrong with the equipment. It was still working. It just couldn't see Bell Tower."

"Any questions?" Dr. Kay searched their faces. They were waiting, thinking. She looked at Jennings. He was staring out of the porthole, oblivious to her. She reminded herself that he had the attention span of a child. "Any questions?" she asked louder.

There were none. She started to speak, but she stopped. The sound was distant and faint. It sounded like helicopters, lots of helicopters. They were growing close. She ignored it and continued. "Good, because we don't have time for them. I believe containment is about to fail, if it hasn't already." She took a deep breath. "I've made up my mind. I'm shutting this project down and calling for Mop Up."

"You can't do that! It's not your decision."

"It is my decision."

Jennings interrupted. He was still leaning against a wall, looking out of a porthole. "Anybody know if we have visitors on the schedule today? There are about five unmarked Hueys hovering out there."

"What the hell? There's no one on the schedule to..."

The explosion came from the north, an Earth-shattering boom that sent vibrations traveling through the steel structure. Metal fragments rained on the hull of the service module. Shrill pings sent echoes from the walls. A second explosion came from the south. Dr. Kay fought to understand what was happening. But it was all happening way too fast.

The chatter of automatic weapons fire erupted all at once from every direction, followed by the thud of grenades.

"Bury the data," she yelled at Jennings as she ran for the air lock. "Do it now."

Her brief marriage to a marine had taught her an important rule. When there's shooting, keep low and keep moving. She exited the outer hatch on her belly and hugged the metal landing. Smoke and cordite stung her nostrils.

She kept her face to the grated surface and peered over the edge. She saw carnage.

Most of the tents were burning or down. The marines were down, all of them, like they'd been shot while standing in formation. Two figures in camouflage fatigues were walking among them, using their pistols on anyone moving. One looked in her direction. She ducked.

More gunfire came from the direction of the Brazilian tents. Her face against grated metal, she slipped back to the landing's edge and peered again into the carnage. Hueys were hovering over the tents and raking them with heavy machine guns. The noise echoed in her skull. She slapped her hands over her ears and watched dozens and dozens of more armed men in camouflage running through gaping holes in the north and south fences.

It would all be over in a few minutes. She knew it. She swung her face toward the microwave dish and saw that it was still standing. The communications tent was also still intact. She did what she would never have believed she could do. She dropped to the ground and ran toward the tent, racing the bullet that she knew would end her life.

She made it barely thirty feet, before she was knocked to the ground. But there'd been no bullet. She'd stumbled over something that had landed her flat on her belly and knocked the wind out of her. She rolled to her side and found herself staring into a face. The Brazilian officer's eyes were open and lifeless. The right side of his mouth was gaping, his brilliant white teeth caked in blood. The left side of his mouth and cheek were gone.

She jumped to her feet and ran. She heard shouting on all sides, felt the presence of someone running behind her.

Gunfire chattered behind her. Bullets whistled over her head, and echoed in her ears. The heat stung her skin, but she kept running.

The shouting grew closer all around her. She reached the tent and tore open the flap. The marine technicians were dead, collapsed over their equipment. Blood was dried around small blue holes in the backs of their heads. They'd been shot execution style while they sat at their stations. She pulled the closest out of his chair and ignored the sound of his body thudding in the dirt.

The radio signal was active. The frequency registered in the LED on the transmitter was already set. She punched her log-in ID and watched the screen register "access accepted." She began to type her password.

Strong hands grabbed her from behind. She caught a flash of wrists twice the size of her own. They felt like steel vices. She felt herself pulled away from the computer. Foul breath touched her. A callused hand buried the whole lower half of her face, as an arm the size of a stove pipe swept across her breasts and crushed her chest. She felt him pull her into him. She flailed wildly. He laughed and spun her around to face him.

He was over six feet tall, broad as a door, and ugly. His automatic weapon was slung over his shoulder. His fatigues were stained in blood that was not his own. A streak of it trailed to the commando knife he wore strapped across his chest. His teeth were rotten, set in a bearded face as ugly and fleshy as a bulldog's. He wore a grenade ring like an ornament in his ear.

She fixed her eyes on his and with all her strength kicked him in the groin. He went down cursing.

She spun back to the computer terminal, catching his movement out of the corner of her eye. He was rolling to his side, unslinging his automatic weapon. Hands trembling, she jammed her message against the keyboard. Two words! She thought of April as she typed them. She thought of the man she'd lost a lifetime ago. She finished the message and watched the software encrypt it.

Out of the corner of her eye, she saw the human bulldog stand and raise his weapon like a club. Dr. Kay reached her finger toward the send button. She never reached it. She felt very little pain. The loud crack vibrated through her whole head. Then there was the warmth that traveled all over. Then blackness.

Bulldog stood over the motionless woman and cursed out loud. He slung his weapon over his shoulder as he heard the other men enter the tent behind him. He turned to face them. The lead man wore camouflage fatigues and paint. He was bald with pale, bloodless cheeks. Steel spectacles and lenses as thick as coke bottles hid eyes that were without brows. The second man wore the uniform of an American marine major. Aviator's glasses hid the second man's eyes. His face was expressionless.

"She wasn't supposed to be hurt," Smith said softly.

"I had to do it. Look at the terminal."

MOP UP was fixed on the screen and awaiting the send button. Smith nodded to himself. He knelt beside the woman, rolled her over on her back, and swept black hair from her face. She was motionless, as if in sleep. Smith stared at her for a long time.

"I used the rifle butt. I didn't hit her hard." Bulldog swallowed as he spoke.

"We'll just have to see, won't we?" Smith stroked the skin of her throat. It was warm, her carotid pulse strong. He rolled open each eyelid. Her eyes were deep, liquid blue. The pupils were not dilated. They reacted normally to light. He rolled her lids closed and watched her breathing. It was regular, deep. "We'll just have to see."

Smith stood and faced the pale, bald man in the thick glasses. "Dr. Steiner, kill the transmitter."

Steiner reached for the transmitter and cut the power.

***

A thousand miles away, within the dark and confined metal walls of the combat information center for the carrier *U.S.S. Nimitz*, a warning alarm sounded. It was a steady, unmistakable series of low beeps. On a computer screen, a message scrolled in red, *FLASH TRAFFIC*. Radioman First-Class Patch O'Reilly acknowledged the traffic and waited for the software to de-encrypt the message.

TIME: 0815 ZULU
TO: T. BISHOP, R. MORGAN (eyes only)
FROM: K. WATERSTONE (ID and password verified)

Procedure called for O'Reilly to wait for the computer to download to a floppy disc. He was to hand said disc to the Officer Of the Day. O'Reilly did not expect to see the message appear on his screen. The message on disc would be seen only by Captain Bishop or Admiral Morgan. O'Reilly waited.

No download occurred.

In mid-broadcast, his receiver indicated the signal was lost. He followed procedure, but was unable to re-establish contact. Within a minute, the Officer of the Day, Lt. Commander Wright, was at his back and briefed on what had happened.

Wright was sweating as he picked up his phone. "Captain, this is the O.O.D. We have a situation." He paused and stared at the blue tile floor. He tried to sound calm, but he was worried. O'Reilly wondered briefly if he was worried about the down signal or worried that he had not executed his job properly.

"Yes, sir. It's Crash Site Alpha Bell Tower. Contact has been lost."

Chapter Three

Thousands of miles north, H.I. Tech knew he was in serious trouble. It was Doc's fault for not listening and for seriously screwing with the one person he should have treated with kid gloves. But kid gloves had never fit Doc. Neither had caution, although Doc would have quibbled with him about what caution meant. So now he, H.I. Tech, was in serious trouble. Go figure. Being in trouble because of Doc was better than being in trouble with Doc. The latter could be life-threatening. Given a choice, H.I. liked the trouble he was in now.

"Do you know why you're here, Mr. Tech?" Vernon Clayfield leaned forward over his antique desk and waited for an answer. But H.I. had none to give him. So Clayfield simply studied him.

Clayfield was wearing shirt sleeves and a loosened tie. His blazer with the Adams Day School patch was hung on the coat rack. Both were bad signs. It meant he had all the time in the world to discuss the matter at hand without fear of interruption. It meant he was going to take his time considering his options and choosing the one that made

him feel the most powerful. And Clayfield liked things that
made him feel powerful. Behind Clayfield, diplomas from
Choate and Harvard were mounted in large frames, bigger than the frame that held his oil painting of Washington
crossing the Delaware and way bigger than his autographed
black and whites of himself with various senators and con-
gressmen on the tennis courts

"Your advisor has made me aware of your absences,
Mr. Tech," Clayfield finally said. "In fact, your absences are
quite numerous."

H.I. knew the answer he wanted to give but knew better
than to give it. No shit, the absences were numerous. And
he didn't like them, either. But the choice had never been
his. H.I. bit his tongue and said the line he'd practiced. "I
was traveling with Doctor Tech. So they were excused, sir."

"Were they indeed?" Clayfield glanced down at a ma-
nila binder where H.I. knew his record to be inscribed in
painful detail. His academic record was not the problem.
Just everything else was the problem. Clayfield opened
the binder. "As I recall, excuses were to be arranged with
me and only me. I don't recall any other arrangement,
Mr. Tech. Do you?"

H.I. knew better than to answer directly. He did his best
to appear concerned without looking scared. But he knew
he was a lousy actor.

"I see here, Mr. Tech, that on September 30 you were
in Geneva for the day. Am I correctly reading your excuse?
You were in Geneva? "

"That's correct."

H.I. looked directly at Clayfield for the first time. Clayfield had cold eyes. His year-round tan made them look

like steel bearings. The rumor was that Clayfield kept a sun lamp in his office so the alumni of Adams Day would think he spent as much time on the golf course as they did. He had to look like one of them because one of his jobs was asking them for endowment money. And it was always easier to give money to what Clayfield was known to call P.LU., *people like us.* He never looked unkempt, except when he was pissed. H.I. knew that when it came to him or Doc, Clayfield had reason to be pissed.

"October 10 through 12, you were Moscow? Is that your story? A three-day absence because you were in Russia?"

"With Doc again. So it wasn't my idea."

"Really? Is that all you can say? Not your idea? " He glanced downward through his reading glasses, looked like he was swallowing vinegar. "Here's my personal pick, Mr. Tech! In November, you were in North Korea for a seven-day absence. North Korea is an outlaw nation and closed to all Americans. Do you earnestly expect me to believe you were there?"

No way would Clayfield believe him. So again, H.I. kept his mouth shut. He watched Clayfield take out his pen, uncap it loudly, and insert a blank paper into his record. Not good. Not good at all. But Clayfield seemed to like it. He began to write an entry.

"You have nothing to add to this, Mr. Tech?"

In fact he had plenty. But nothing that would solve his problem with Clayfield, so again he stuck to his practiced answer. "There's nothing here that wasn't in the arrangement."

"It's an arrangement that has not been kept. As I recall, your father was to consult me personally prior to your absences. But that hasn't been happening."

"That's because he's delegated it to me."

"Really! He left it up to you, the job of notifying me?"

"It wasn't a responsibility I liked, either. But Doc was in a hurry every time. So he delegated the things he thought were unimportant."

"Did I hear you correctly? Did you say notifying me was unimportant?" Clayfield stopped writing. "The arrangement was equitable, Mr. Tech. Your father takes you on his so-called professional trips. I look the other way."

H.I. kept his mouth shut. It wasn't time to use his ace in the hole. And he wasn't sure how Clayfield would react. He thought about telling Clayfield the truth. But there was no way Clayfield would believe him. No one would.

"And why was it that you did not notify me, Mr. Tech?"

"Because I was always in a hurry too. Doc probably told you these trips are always emergencies."

"He called them business trips, Mr. Tech. Scientific matters was what he said."

"Did he say anything about crisis management?" H.I. held his breath and thought of all the not-very-nice places his father had dragged him. He thought about all the not-very-nice people in those places and how some of them would like to see Doc dead. He thought about how they'd like to see him dead too. But there was no point in telling Clayfield about all that. Clayfield would never believe it anyway. "Trust me, crisis is the operative word every time. Scientific crisis."

"Bound to happen, I guess. You were bound to abuse the arrangement," Clayfield said. "Certainly nothing I can do about it at this point. But I certainly do not believe that your father, a man with five degrees, delegated anything to you. Nor do I believe that your account of where you've been all of these times is honest in the least."

"You think I'm lying?"

"I know you're lying. I'll leave it to your father to determine where you've been all of these times."

"He'll confirm that I've been with him. When are you going to talk to him?"

"I'm not going to talk to him." Clayfield leaned backward in his chair, clenched fists on his desk. "I have the board to worry about. And there is no way to bury this now, even if you are telling the truth. The board will not be pleased at any of this, not pleased one bit. They demand everyone play by the same rules—even Dr. Tech, a man with five degrees! This will mean expulsion for you and the end of a big headache for me."

Expulsion! The thought of it sent a shiver through H.I. Anger followed. There was no fricking way he was going to let Clayfield flush his future down the toilet. And by future, he did not mean the academic kind. He had a fricking 4.0 GPA in spite of Doc's dragging his ass off on one damn excursion after another. And if he didn't continue his studies at Adams Day, he'd bloody well continue them somewhere else. No one asked where you went to high school anyway. They probably asked where you went to college, but what they really wanted to know was what you could do for them. And H.I. Tech knew he'd be able to do plenty. So he didn't give a damn about whether his academic future was at Adams Day. What he cared about was being near someone else who attended Adams Day. And that someone else was still April Waterstone. She wouldn't answer his calls or come to the door. So the best he could hope for was seeing her at school. And no one was going to take that away from him. Not Doc and not Clayfield.

"Your Adams Day career ends after final exams next week, Mr. Tech."

Time to set up the ace in the hole, H.I. told himself. "I don't want my career to end, sir."

"What you want is of no consequence. The board likes those who play by the rules."

Time to play the ace in the hole, H.I. knew. Now or never. He stared at Clayfield a full thirty seconds before speaking. "I'm guessing the board would want you to play by the rules too, wouldn't they, sir. I don't think they'll be too happy with your part in my absences or the private deal you made with Doc."

"What did you say?"

"You heard me."

No one ever got thrown out of Vernon Clayfield's office. He never got loud. That was because there was always the possibility that alumni or prospective new parents might be out in the hall. He'd just say the meeting was over and show whomever he was addressing to the door. He always liked to shake hands at that point and then simply send the target of his venom back to class without watching him walk away. That afternoon he let H.I. Tech go without a handshake and closed the door immediately.

The hallway was empty, and the door to the science lab was open as H.I. passed it. He hated that damn lab. It represented everything that had intruded in his life. It wasn't that he really wanted anything big for his life. He just wanted it be ordinary. Ordinary would have been cool. But being Doc's son made ordinary impossible. H.I. was still thinking about ordinary when he passed the plainclothes cop.

H.I. knew he was a cop right away. He was a big guy in a beat-up overcoat and a cheap suit, looking at the world like everyone in it was doing something wrong. He was aware of his surroundings in a manner that said he expected everyone to be afraid of him. Definitely a cop, H.I. told himself. Waiting for someone, obviously, but no one of importance to H.I. or anyone H.I. knew.

H.I. brushed by him without more than a glance.

The door to his classroom was open. Phil Bagley was visible from the hall and writing on his blackboard. Bagley was gray and balding, had a scruffy mustache stained from coffee. He looked like a janitor in a bad tweed jacket. He taught math.

"A moment of silence, everyone!" Bagley saw H.I. and turned from the board. "Mr. Tech has decided to grace us with his presence."

"Where was it this time, H.I., Tangiers?" The taunt came from the back.

"Nah, it was probably Saigon." This one came from closer to the front.

Bagley yelled at everyone to shut up. He went back to his board. H.I. moved to the back of the class. Getting there, he had to run the usual gauntlet, mostly stares but also the usual whispers saying hi. They weren't meant to be a greeting. They were a play on the name that he hated, a name none of them even knew. So he was always called by his initials as if H.I. were "hi". That was okay. He considered it better than having his name known. And somewhere down the line, he'd be changing his name anyway. He'd change it to something really ordinary, like Harry or Hank Irving. What could be more ordinary and anonymous than Hank or Harry?

The last hi came from a six-foot, two-inch, fair-haired Neanderthal named Buddy Stagmire. Buddy's smile always looked so real. It hid his true nature. He was saving H.I. a seat across from him and directly behind April Waterstone. She saw H.I. heading for it. She wasn't happy.

H.I. shot her his best smile. She flicked her chin in the other direction. Buddy Stagmire watched the two of them and grinned. It was one of those moments that always seemed to give Stagmire pleasure, especially when he could set them up. H.I. told himself that actually Neanderthal was not a fair description of Buddy Stagmire. First, it wasn't fair to Neanderthals, because they probably weren't all assholes. And second, it wasn't fair to Buddy, either. He was actually damn smart even though he was an asshole. In fact, given a chance, H.I. Tech would have traded places with Buddy Stagmire in a heartbeat. Buddy was smart enough to get a good GPA without looking like a nerd, smart enough to get other assholes to do his dirty work without getting caught, smart enough to break football training without pissing off the coaches, and smart enough to still be going out with the someone who never wanted to look at H.I. again.

H.I. took his seat behind April. She shot Buddy a look that could kill and then snapped away quickly so she could avoid eye contact with H.I. H.I. felt the pain only for a second. He was getting used to it. And besides, he knew things were his fault. Still he could have looked at April forever. Sitting there he would have, but from the back of the classroom, Jefferson Parrish shook his head. April sensed the communication between the two. It set her off.

She straightened a skirt that was way too short and hiking up her thigh. Then she crossed her legs. April Waterstone had perfect legs, dancer's legs. She turned toward him slowly. She was beautiful even when she was pissed. No creases under her eyes this time. They were blue storms.

"Get out of my life, Tech."

"I'm already out of your life. And not liking it."

"You have nobody to blame but yourself." She turned away with snap of her chin and a flick of blonde hair. Classic Waterstone moves.

"Lover's quarrel, Miss Waterstone?" Phil Bagley turned from the blackboard.

"Just a quarrel," she answered.

There was a lot of laughter but only a few sneers. Buddy shot H.I. all the false empathy he could muster. For April he saved a simple shrug. She didn't buy his act. Didn't matter though. H.I. knew she would still be going out with him. Go figure.

Bagley turned back to his blackboard. He had chalk all over his tweed jacket. "This one problem will keep some of you busy for an hour. Take your time. It's a whole test grade."

Notebooks opened at all of the other desks around H.I. The notebooks were required and provided to all Adams Day students at a considerable markup. Nothing but the best money could buy at Adams Day. Keyboards started clacking. H.I. left his alone. He stared at the board for a brief moment.

"X squared," He said. He regretted saying it as soon as he opened my mouth.

"How's that, Mr. Tech?"

"X squared. Your answer is X squared."

"Correct, Mr. Tech." Bagley put what muscle he had into the eraser as he attacked the blackboard to undo his rows of equations. He spoke like he was seriously pissed. "You'll have a harder problem, courtesy of Mr. Tech."

Lots of groans. H.I. ignored most but not all.

"Thanks a lot, asshole," April said. "I mean you, Tech. Not Bagley."

"Do you have a problem, Miss Waterstone?" Bagley stopped writing.

"Big time."

"Take a seat up front, Miss Waterstone. And you, Mr. Tech, move to the back. Don't let me hear from you again."

"Yes, sir."

"That's hearing from you, Mr. Tech. I don't want to hear from you."

The class broke into applause. Bagley shut them up. H.I. moved to the back row next to Jefferson Parrish. Jefferson leaned over and whispered, "Back of the bus, baby."

"Bullshit," H.I. whispered back. "You never had to ride in the back of the bus in your life."

"But I know what it must have felt like," he said. "You do too."

"No, with me it's not racial. It's personal."

H.I. rubbed his eyes, making Bagley and his blackboard become a blur. He heard Bagley scribbling furiously, talking as he did. "Your new test, courtesy of Mr. Tech, is a practical math exercise. I don't know how many of you remember RM 1999, the comet that is supposed to have hit our dear planet last summer. Well, we're going to use your considerable math skills to calculate the energy of RM 1999's impact and come up with a model that explains why it didn't blow the doors off this entire little world of ours."

Good luck, H.I. thought. There was no model that could explain what had happened to RM 1999 on impact. Doc had said so himself and then said the whole thing had probably been a cover for something the government didn't want anyone to know anything about. Or maybe all of the observations leading up to its impact had been faulty. It was hard to know because Raymond Marsden, the astronomer who'd raised the alarm was still out of the public eye and not talking.

H.I. let his gaze drift to the cover of his math book, which the publisher had done up liken an endless field of stars. The pi symbol was in the right hand bottom corner, which seemed appropriate. Like his life, pi had value with no fixed solution. H.I. fell asleep staring at the cover of his book. Endless stars with blackness in between.

The bell woke him roughly, left his eyes hurting from interruption in the wrong stage of sleep. The class was empty. April was gone. So were his books. H.I. knew where both were headed. He moved to the hall and cut through a crowd clad in blazers with Adams Day patches. Under the far exit sign, he caught a glimpse of a familiar blonde head nestled on Buddy Stagmire's shoulder. Buddy was carrying two sets of books, and H.I. knew one of the sets had to be his bound for the dumpster.

H.I. closed the distance fast. Buddy was taking his time walking with April. She had her thumb inside one of his belt loops. H.I. walked faster. Within ten feet of her, H.I. saw April drop her magazine, a copy of *Elle* in French. As H.I. stepped over it, he looked down. The cover model was throwing a pouty smile over her shoulder. Blonde hair worthy of Rapunzel was falling down her naked back and splaying over her buttocks. The caption read *La Riviere de l'ete; toute des problems du monde finis.* H.I. picked it up, rolled it like one of his newspapers, and kept walking. Within five feet of April, he slammed into Clayfield. Clayfield took the magazine.

"Really, Mr. Tech? All of the problems of the world finished?"

H.I. shrugged.

"Yours are just starting." Clayfield forced a smile. "Next week are your finals. And then you'll want to say good-bye."

Clayfield returned the magazine to H.I., smiled coldly, and walked away. His expensive shoes clicked on the tile as if he were wearing taps. H.I. gave him some distance, then spun and ran through the double doors into the parking lot.

Outside the spaces reserved for Most Outstanding Seniors were along the walkway beyond the spaces belonging to administration. In the closest space, April was just settling into the passenger seat of Buddy's jeep and reaching for her door. H.I. began to run. She turned in his direction.

For a second their eyes met. Hers were blue storms. His were lost. Buddy reached across her and slammed her door shut. H.I. froze in place. He watched.

Buddy Stagmire's jeep backed into the lot, stopped abuptly, and spun as it accelerated toward the school entrance. It stopped briefly at the dumpster, then burned rubber as it shot out of sight between the twin stone columns embossed with the good name of Adams Day School.

A plain sedan followed on Buddy's tail. H.I. didn't pay much attention to the car, just the driver. It was the big man with a pockmarked face, the cop. H.I. watched him flick a cigarette out of his window and accelerate. The cop and his car vanished.

It was getting cold fast, starting to drizzle. H.I. kept the *Elle*, decided to leave his books in the dumpster, and headed back into school to get his coat. Just inside the glass doors, Jefferson was waiting for him.

"He didn't have them this time, man." Jefferson handed H.I. his books. "Stagmire was just jacking with you."

"Glad I didn't climb into the dumpster."

"She leave with him again?"

"Same as everyday."

"That's ugly, baby."

"Yeah." H.I. looked at the *Elle* and almost threw it away. Instead he tucked it under his arm. Later he would wonder what would have happened if April had not dropped that magazine and he had not picked it up. Probably she wouldn't even be alive. Later he would tell himself that life was like that, often turning on one event.

Chapter Four

"You real sure about this, Ramsey?"

"Very sure, Senator. Communication with the crash site cannot be reestablished. The carrier group still hasn't heard from its marines. Our Brazilian counterparts are nervous. They want to know what's going on."

Senator Orton Bledso turned to the window. His corner office allowed him an unobstructed view of both the Capital and the Supreme Court. When the news was bad, he chose to look southwest. That direction gave him a view of the Capital and beyond its dome, a look at the tip of the Washington Monument. When the news was bad, he stroked the white handlebar mustache that reminded his voters of Mark Twain. In his state, the resemblance was important.

It was late afternoon. It was gray and wet. His view was not pretty. He turned to face Ramsey. "Of course they want to know! Bell Tower came down in their backyard. They let us handle it because we had the know-how. Now communication is dead, and we can't tell them shit."

Bledso cursed under his breath. It was to be his last term in the Senate. He wanted to retire without a stain, and now it looked like that wasn't going to happen. He turned his six foot two inch frame and poured himself a Bourbon and branch water from the crystal decanter on his Renaissance desk.

Bledso took a good look at Ramsey, made him to be somewhere between thirty-five and forty. From the standpoint of Bledso's upbringing, Ramsey had acceptable skin, merely burnt almond in shade. But Ramsey's eyes were black as a swamp bog and just as unfathomable. And Ramsey carried himself secretively, his unassuming posture giving no clue to the endless physical training Bledso knew him to have endured. To Bledso, Ramsey looked like just another suit who might never be noticed in a crowd. In DC offices, he might easily be mistaken for an aide, a clerk, a secretary, anything but what he was. Anything but CIA. Bledso wished he'd never met him.

The first meeting had taken place five months earlier, the day after Bell Tower had gone down in the Amazon. The appointment book had not specified who Ramsey represented, just listed him as a lobbyist and booked him in the last afternoon spot. Afterward, Bledso had stayed late and had a lot to drink.

"Anything from the satellites?" Bledso took a big swallow of his very expensive bourbon.

"Site's socked in by clouds. We've got infrared only. Shows lots of activity. Lots of people down there. More than there should be."

"I want a fly-over. Tell the *Nimitz*."

"Won't help. Site's real socked in. Clouds go all the way down."

"Any chance of getting any more of our people in on the ground?"

"Like I said, our counterparts are damn nervous. They feel they already went pretty far just letting in the one platoon of marines. Right now they just want answers."

"Are you telling me the Brazilians don't know about the down communication?"

"I'm not telling you anything, Senator. You still have plausible deniability. So does the President."

Bledso finished his drink in a gulp. He thought of ETRAC and how it had come under his tent through the Senate Intelligence Committee. That first afternoon five months ago he'd been told by Ramsey that his senatorial signature was already on ETRAC documents and memorandums. They had been for years. His and only his signature. At the time, Bledso had conceded that a lot of paper and a lot of small agencies came under his tent. There simply wasn't time to oversee them all. Everything was a brief or a memo.

Five months ago he'd told Ramsey he'd never believed in extraterrestrial life. He still didn't. But he did believe that objects falling from space could present a threat to human kind. In the twentieth century, all logical thinkers had to accept that possibility.

ETRAC was an interdepartmental organization. That much Bledso knew. Its reach went as far as the National Security Agency, Space Command, the Air Force, NASA, and the CIA. Maybe its reach stretched into other agencies too. But there was no way for Bledso to know. What came to him was only the limited information some person or maybe some panel deemed he should know. Bledso was supposed to be providing oversight for ETRAC. But Bledso knew only what Ramsey told him.

Bledso didn't trust Ramsey, saw him as too calm. Calm was the measure of men who had none of their own chips in the game. If things went bad, Ramsey would simply disappear somewhere inside the Beltway. Bledso would be by himself at a microphone facing an investigation. Bledso wished the whole thing had waited another year. Then it would have been out of his hands. He cursed again.

"I will have to tell the president, Ramsey. He will make this some sort of international crisis."

"I have an alternative."

"What's that, Ramsey?

Ramsey paced briefly. He made it a point never to sit when he was in Senator Bledso's office. He made it a point never to stand near a window. "The obvious solution is an outside consultant. Go private."

"Who'd you have in mind?"

"Dr. Tech! Dr. Jules Verne Tech."

"Tech's a damn pain in the ass. But I like your thinking." Bledso decided against a second drink. He was feeling better. He sat in his plush leather chair and let himself take in his whole view. The whole view included the Supreme Court building with its imposing columns. A minute earlier, the columns had made him think of a prison. He turned back to Ramsey. "Dr. Tech. Outstanding idea."

Ramsey nodded. He never smiled, not even when his ideas were commended.

"This time I want a security team hugging him like a silk suit on a New Orleans pimp." Bledso stood and began pacing again. "I don't want that maverick acting on his own."

"I'll take charge of him myself."

"I said a team, Ramsey."

"Alex Malone is en route from Langley."

"Outstanding."

Bledso sat down again. He looked at his decanter and his empty glass.

"There's one more matter, Ramsey."

"Are you talking about Doctor Marsden?"

"Yes. How did you know?"

"I know. That's all that matters."

Bledso leaned forward in his chair and drummed his desk. "Marsden's staying at the Marriot. He wants to talk about Bell Tower. I've broken four appointments with him. I don't want to talk with him."

"You won't have to talk with him, Senator."

"Why's that?" Bledso started to pour himself a second drink.

"Because he's been explained the facts of life, and he understands. You won't hear from him again."

Bledso pushed away his decanter. He felt better again. He looked at the Supreme Court building with its imposing columns. The drizzle had stopped, but it was still gray.

"Outstanding," he muttered as he rocked back in his plush leather chair.

Chapter Five

The traffic around the Beltway was bad. Ramsey took forty-five minutes to get to Bethesda, park his sedan, and find his way into the small office at the NIH. By that time he'd missed Dr. Jules Verne Tech. It took Ramsey another twenty minutes to get to Methodist Hospital and another ten minutes to find the right auditorium. Ramsey let himself in through the back door and settled in the dark, leaning against the wall and draping his raincoat over his arm. He wasn't noticed.

Around him all of the men and women were young, most dressed in surgical scrubs and all of them dressed in white lab coats. Most of the lab coats were wrinkled, many of them soiled. Some of the wearers sat on the floor. Others slumped in seats. All of them looked tired. More than one was fighting sleep. Ramsey knew they were mostly house staff, meaning interns and residents. Some of them were medical students. The students wore waist-length white coats, pockets stuffed with instruments, tourniquets, and small books; they looked alert but nervous. Ramsey looked for Doc but couldn't find him.

Below Ramsey the carpeted floor sloped down to a small stage. The front row was occupied by older men and women, most of them wearing well-worn suits and ties. Their heads were craned upward toward the podium that shared the stage with a row of lighted X-ray boxes. Stepping to the podium, a single resident waited for a signal to start. He badly needed a shave. He looked like he'd slept in his clothes. Responding to the nod of a man in the front row, the resident keyed the microphone with a loud whine and introduced himself as Dr. Davis before dimming the lights even further. He spoke nervously.

"Today's case is D.M., a twenty-year-old hemophiliac with an eight-week history of fever and temps of 101 to 102." Dr. Davis coughed, fumbled with papers, and continued. "D.M. also complains of night sweats and a weight loss of fifteen pounds. He denies headache, sore throat, cough, nausea, diarrhea, flank pain, dysuria, arthralgia, or rash. He has no history of drug or alcohol abuse. On exam, he appears chronically ill, but his exam is otherwise unremarkable."

Ramsey tried to search the front row. His view was blocked so he watched Dr. Davis call for the slide projector and grab a laser pointer. The pointer's spot began to dance along scrolls of test data displayed on an overhead screen. Dr. Davis mumbled and stumbled though the results, then forced confidence and enthusiasm into his voice for the finish. "In summary, his blood work including his HIV screen is negative. So are his films and CT. Blood cultures are pending. Echocardiogram shows normal valves. And again though on physical he has no murmur or petechia, my guess is SBE."

"Is that what you're learning in this program, Dr. Davis? How to guess?" The question came from the front row. It was a deep voice with just a hint of the old south, slow enough to be polite and intimidating at the same time. Ramsey knew the voice well.

So did everyone around Ramsey. Their whispering stopped. None of them were asleep any more, or even fighting sleep for that matter. All of them were glued to Dr. Davis, watching him as if expecting an execution. At the podium, Dr. Davis began stammering. "SBE, subacute bacterial endocarditis, for those of you who are medical students, is the most common cause of a prolonged and unexplained fever. It's been our experience at this institution where we have a large referral service. And it's been my experience as well."

"You're a first-year resident, Dr. Davis," the voice with the southern accent continued even slower, filling with sarcasm. "You don't have experience."

Dr. Davis was smart enough not to respond. He froze in place, as a few brief laughs swept across the auditorium. He focused his attention directly down into the front row.

"On the other hand, Dr. Davis, I do have experience. What might that be?"

"Your experience, Dr. Tech?"

"Yes, let's hear what the word *experience* might mean."

"Yes, sir. You hold doctorates in physics, biochemistry, and medicine. You are boarded in both internal medicine and surgery. You hold two chairs at Georgetown, run a fellowship at the NIH, and are an attending at this hospital."

"That's correct. It appears you've at least assimilated something while here."

In the front row, the speaker, Dr. Jules Verne Tech, stood up straight and tall. He was powerful in the shoulders, flat in the belly, and serious in the face. Ramsey knew Dr. Tech's was a face many considered handsome. Maybe it was a matter of his confidence or maybe his face was angular in just the right way. Steel gray hair added a look of command. That he always looked in need of a barber was the only feature out of synch with the near military precision with which he climbed to the podium. There was no white coat on him. Instead his suit was dark blue, custom-fitted and expensive like his Italian shoes and the gray turtleneck under his suit jacket. He looked like a man dressed by his wife or at least taught how to dress by his wife. In Dr. Tech's case, the wife was long gone. That had been her choice.

Dr. Jules Verne Tech, "Doc" to a selected few, climbed to the X-ray boxes and studied them only briefly. He spoke slowly, forcing even more of the deep south into his words. "This looks like about ten million dollars worth of lab work and ten cents worth of doctor."

The auditorium broke into laughter but got quiet again quickly. It always got that way when Doc had something to say. "There's a linear infiltrate in the apex of your negative film. This kid has TB." Doc turned to Dr. Davis. "Tell me, doctor. Didn't you do a TB skin test?"

"We did. It was negative."

"Then this kid's also anergic. That's bad. Who okayed this case?"

"I did, Dr. Tech." A white-coated figure, this one slightly built and prematurely bald, stood in the second row.

"Didn't you bother to review this case before presentation?"

The little bald doctor in the second row didn't answer.

"You are the chief resident, aren't you? It's your responsibility to supervise Dr. Davis, is it not?"

"Yes, sir."

"Is this patient in isolation?"

The bald doctor deferred to Dr. Davis. Dr. Davis stammered. "The patient's family had some input on that, and we didn't have an indication."

"You do know what to do at this point, do you not?"

"Yes, sir. We put him in isolation. Stain his sputum for acid-fast. Start double drugs."

Doc turned to the auditorium. He was angry. "This diagnosis should have been made on the first X-ray. There's a lesson here. I've said it before. I guess I have to say it again. When you hear the sound of hooves, think of horses, not zebras."

The auditorium was quiet.

"Grand rounds adjourned."

Ramsey left the auditorium ahead of Doc and put on his rain coat. Outside the building, Ramsey found an alcove facing the reserved parking lot and positioned himself so he could see Doc's parking place. Ramsey knew the spot and knew Doc's black BMW. Ramsey waited, but not long. Ramsey caught up with him before he climbed behind the wheel. But Doc sensed Ramsey's presence before he even turned.

"You should have called first, Ramsey. You know I like a heads-up. "

"There wasn't time, doctor. We have a zebra."

Chapter Six

Ramsey drove a plain gray sedan with a serial number under the driver's side window and with government tags front and back. Doc sat in the passenger seat and kept one eye on Ramsey while listening to the local news on the radio. The announcer said that a scientist had fallen to his death from the eleventh floor of the Marriott. The police were calling it suicide. Doc missed the victim's name.

"You mind, Doctor?" Ramsey turned off the radio.

They headed south into DC, crossed the Potomac, and skirted a large lagoon. The building they entered was built on a mud flat once known as "Hell's Bottom." Some might have thought the name was deserved. But others knew the work that went on inside that building demanded considerable sacrifice on the part of those who worked there.

The Pentagon is made of five pentagonal buildings joined by ten spoke corridors to form one town-sized, five-sided structure enclosing a five-acre courtyard. The building's outside circumference is a full mile. The Pentagon is five stories above ground and two stories below. At any one time, twenty-three thousand people are working inside.

There are lots of dull jobs to be done: shuffling paper work
and going to meetings. There are administrators and sec-
retaries and mail room people and computer nerds. Most
are ordinary folks who could be working anywhere. But
there are also the others who are highly trained and working under all kinds of pressure. They can't talk about what
they do. They don't get paid well. They don't get to per-
form in front of cheering crowds, and they don't get to pro-
mote sports equipment bearing their names. They don't
get their photos in *People* magazine, and they don't appear
on *Letterman*. They face constant change in equipment and
situations and protocols. They do a lot of homework, make
some very tough calls, and maybe grow some ulcers. When
they screw up, lots of people get hurt. So the best of them
worry a lot. Doc remembered these things every time he
entered the building.

There are no elevators inside the Pentagon, just ramps,
stairs, and escalators. Doc insisted on stairs, nearly outpacing
Ramsey. Doc's and Ramsey's destination was a windowless
room just off a ramp at the northwest point. Had the room
had a view, it would have been of the Arlington National
Cemetery. Ramsey might have even looked out of a window,
looked at all of those graves, and been a worrier too, Doc
told himself. But on second thought, he doubted it.

The room had been scheduled for Ramsey's use only
two hours earlier. The faces of the Air Force officers, NASA
engineers, and NSA people were known to him personally.
They were not known to Doc. Doc wouldn't have cared anyway. His attention was on the satellite photo.

"It was shear, blind luck that we got this one frame,"
Ramsey said.

"Not one of your best," Doc said.

"Not one of our satellites," Ramsey responded.

The environmental satellite had been obtaining data on the rain forest, part of a study on global warming. It didn't have the kind of optics meant for snooping. Had it been an NSA satellite, things would have been different. The NSA, the National Security Agency, had the optics to photograph license plates from orbit. The environmental satellite had taken the equivalent of a look-down from a mile. Photo enlargement and enhancement had produced the grainy copy that Doc inspected.

Doc looked at the photo for a long time. He cleaned his glasses. "Why didn't you change the orbit of one your own and have another look?"

"We did."

"Where are your photos?"

"You'll see them. You won't like them."

In the grainy environmental satellite photo, the trees were felled for miles in an expanding butterfly pattern ending in a crater. The crater was wedge-shaped, shallow at one end, and deep at the other. Its length was slightly more than a mile from impact point to its deep, flat end. The thing that dug the crater was still intact in the deep end.

It looked like a drop of mercury. That's all. Just a drop of mercury in the corner of a grainy photo taken from above. The drop was a perfect half-sphere with flat surface down and round surface up. There were no shadows under its edges. It appeared to hug the ground. Doc judged it to be the size of a small building.

"One of your toys fall out of orbit?" Doc asked.

"Not this time. You're looking at down at Object Alpha Bell Tower. You can see from the crater shape that it was in level flight when it impacted. As best as can be determined, it came down intact."

"Where are your photos?" Doc asked. "The ones I won't like?"

Ramsey handed them to him. They showed nothing but dense clouds.

"These must have been taken days later. You guys were slow," Doc said.

"No. We were fast. These were taken by one of ours only ninety minutes after impact."

Doc whistled and thumbed through serial shots photographed with less magnification. They showed the dark clouds spreading like a flat, dense roof across the rain forest. Within an hour, the dark cloud covered twenty square miles of jungle. On infrared, the object's heat signature lit the cloud's center. It was hotter than the signatures of forest life. Serial shots over the next forty-eight hours showed changes. Bad changes.

"Everything—plants, animals, even bacteria for all we know—was dead within two days of impact," Ramsey explained.

"Radiation?"

"We think worse."

Doc put down the folder and rubbed his eyes. Ramsey continued. "Our people sealed off the area at once, but…"

"Who's the team leader?" Doc interrupted.

"Kay Waterstone."

Doc knew he looked stunned. For once, even he was speechless, and he knew Ramsey had picked up on his reaction right away. Must have been the CIA training. Ramsey spoke softly. "You had to have known she was working on something important, Doctor."

"When do I leave?"

"Immediately. But there's something else you need to know." Ramsey told Doc that all communication with Crash Site Alpha Bell Tower was lost, told him the implications and what might be done as a remedy. Doc didn't like what he heard.

Less than a minute later, Ramsey was guiding Doc along one of the Pentagon's spoke corridors. Two Air Force officers followed. One ramp below ground level on the north courtyard side, they entered an empty hallway. Doc knew where they were going.

"The time table is real tight on this one." Ramsey fidgeted with his ear phone.

"You should have called me sooner," Doc responded.

Ramsey didn't react. He fidgeted with his ear phone again, then turned to Doc. "Malone's here. I'll introduce you."

"I'm not traveling with any CIA goblins."

"I'm your first goblin. Alex Malone is the other. We're both professionals. Malone has had ten years in the field. And she knows the terrain at Bell Tower like a native."

"Let me guess! Crew cut, bad suit, and a ten-cc brain."

Doc followed Ramsey into an office vestibule and paused for a second when he heard the sound of the news on TV. A local anchor was reporting on a suicide at the Marriott Hotel. Doc stepped into the office just ahead of Ramsey, then froze.

"Hello, Dr. Tech. I'm Alex Malone."

The introduction came from a young woman seated alone in the office. Doc found her leaning back in a chair with her legs crossed on top of a desk. Immediately she muted the television, stood, and extended a strong, slender arm. Her grip was soft but firm. She held Doc's hand longer than she needed, stood closer than she needed.

Doc judged her at five-three, but thought she looked taller in her heels. Hard to judge height in heels, Doc told himself. He looked down into her small face. Malone had delicate cheekbones and a sensuous mouth. Her hair was copper colored, pulled back severely. Rimless glasses gave her the look of a school teacher. Behind the glasses, fine eyebrows arched over inquisitive green eyes. Doc sensed something cold in the eyes.

"I don't need the CIA," was all Doc said.

"You didn't tell him?" Malone spoke to Ramsey.

"Some! Not all." Ramsey leaned against a wall. " I was waiting for you."

"Let me tell you why you very much do need the CIA, Doctor." Malone raised her face into Doc's and tried to judge his reaction. None. She continued. "This loss of communication may just be technical, or Alpha Bell Tower's security may have been compromised. Our people may not even be in control."

"My job still doesn't require the CIA."

Malone looked at Ramsey, who had moved to the coffee machine next to the refrigerator. He motioned a cup toward her. "I think it's fresh."

"Heavy cream. One ice cube. No sugar." She accepted the coffee.

Out of the corner of his eye, Doc glanced at the TV. Something familiar caught his attention. Not the street crowd or the dead body being loaded into an ambulance. The familiar thing flashed again, a photo of a distinguished middle-aged man.

"We are on the same side in this thing." Malone softened her tone, leaned back against the desk, and crossed one leg over the other. She took off her glasses and cleaned her lenses. Her eyes became almost innocent. "So I'm going to tell you about my job."

Doc nodded, kept his eye on the TV. A file tape showed the distinguished middle-aged man, alive and talking with Larry King. The man's photo froze and became superimposed with captions, the year of his birth and death. Ramsey stepped behind Malone and clicked the television off.

Malone replaced her glasses and continued. "The aircraft carrier *Nimitz* is on station off the coast of Brazil, and it is waiting on what I report. I'd like to report that you fixed things at Alpha Bell Tower. That sound good to you?"

"And if I can't? Fix things?" Doc asked.

"Then I make choices. One of which could be Mop Up." She explained what Mop Up was.

"Mop Up! An option of last resort." Doc responded.

"Then let's you and Ramsey and I see that it isn't needed. Sound good to you?"

Doc didn't answer. In his own mind, he was already ten steps ahead of Malone and thinking hard about Kay Waterstone.

Chapter Seven

Being knocked out is not like being asleep. It's dreamless and black, and all the time you are at the mercy of the world around you. When you come to, there can be brief amnesia and disorientation. And if you are lucky, there is no permanent brain damage. Dr. Kay was lucky.

She regained consciousness five hours after Crash Sight Alpha Bell Tower was taken. The first sensation made her think she was dreaming. She heard classical music, mixed somehow with the distant beating of helicopter blades. She opened her eyes. The light seemed blinding. Her ears rang.

She shut her eyes and tried to move. Something held her in place.

Her lab coat was gone. Her wrists were bound behind her back. Her shoes and socks were gone, and her ankles were bound tight, skin to skin. She was lying in the open, on a tarpaulin. How? Why? She fought panic, and then she remembered. It all came back to her.

There'd been the attack and the killing. All of the marines dead, shot as if in formation. The Brazilians were also probably all dead. Killed by who? Why? Her mind began to clear. She knew the why part.

She raised her head and saw the twisted hole that the explosives had ripped in the cyclone fence. She heard digging from the other direction. She rolled to face the sound. Fifty feet away from her and under guard, the Jivanos Indians were digging a slit trench. Just beyond the Indians, the dead marines were spread out on the Earth. The flies were already swarming.

Another memory came back like an ice pick, stabbing her deep in her center. It wasn't a real memory, just what she thought it might have been. A bombed out barracks in Beirut and the sorting out of dead marines, one of whom was her husband. Only he wasn't buried in a mass grave dug at gun point. He came home in a steel box draped in colors, heralded by an honor guard.

She struggled against her bonds, felt them dig into her flesh. Nothing loosened. She collapsed and heard the music again, told herself she was imagining it. But it was real. Somebody was playing Wagner on the PA system, letting it drift slowly and melodically from speakers mounted on light poles along the wrecked cyclone fence. The music evoked a dread from something she could not remember. She fought tears. A nearby guard heard her and spun to face her.

"Hey, Bulldog! She's awake, man." The accent was likely South African.

A second guard joined the first. Dr. Kay thought she remembered the second one, the one called Bulldog. He was a big man with a fleshy face and a grenade ring in his ear. She stopped crying and tensed her muscles as he unsheathed his commando knife and bent over her. He cut the rope binding her ankles and jerked her to her feet. She was unsteady for a second.

"No tricks, my little China." Bulldog's accent was definitely South African. She knew "my little China" was Africaans for friend. Bulldog held the knife in front of her face and grinned wide. His teeth and breath were foul. She did remember him.

Bulldog gave her a firm push and walked behind her. She took a last look at the dead marines and let herself cry again. Two huey helicopters roared in just over her head. Beyond her they nosed up and hovered over men working among burned tree stumps. The stumps stretched all of the way to the east horizon and marked the terrain scorched by Bell Tower in its last second before impact.

Bell Tower! She remembered Bell Tower and stopped crying. She asked herself if her coworkers had buried the Bell Tower data in time. She tried to look in the direction of the complex, but Bulldog gave another shove.

She stumbled forward, as she heard a loud whistle. She twisted her head east, saw the camouflaged men running for cover. The helicopters were climbing fast. Explosions followed instantly. They rang in her ears. She felt heat from the blasts, shut her eyes, and tried to crouch. Bulldog kept her upright with his grip. She caught her breath and opened her eyes to Bulldog's laugh.

Toward the east, fragments from blasted tree trunks rained down through a thick cloud of jungle dirt. Under guard and carrying tools, Jivanos Indians moved into the blast sight. Tractors driven by men in camouflage followed.

Bulldog pushed her past the control complex. The main air lock was open. All of her coworkers were seated on the muddy ground and were under guard. Jennings tried to make eye contact. He turned and showed Dr. Kay that his hands were bound behind his back.

"Move along, my China." Bulldog almost sent her flying. She recovered her footing and stumbled forward. The music became louder and operatic, a single chord repeating over and over in sweeping movements. Definitely Wagner! She shuddered. She hated Wagner. His operas were beautiful but also frightening. Now she remembered why they induced so much dread, a rainy college day spent listening to his music as she watched a documentary about Nazi death camps. .

Bulldog pushed her toward newly dug bunkers south of the control complex. They were nearly complete, and Dr. Kay told herself she must have been unconscious for a long time. There were armed men in camouflage everywhere. Dr. Kay tried to estimate their number, promising herself it would be useful information later. She guessed over two hundred, all of them disciplined. Some were giving orders, as if they were officers. Some shouting was in English, the rest in an Eastern European language, likely Russian.

Bulldog guided her down into the darkness of the largest bunker. She felt a carpet under her feet. It overlay a wooden floor. She let her eyes adjust slowly in the dark and listened as the music disc changed on a CD player. Another Wagner opera began. It was almost hypnotic.

She blinked and made out the shadow of a man seated in a swivel chair. His back was toward her, as he clicked the lights along a panel of mirrors. Beyond the mirrors, she recognized surgical lamps.

"It's time for us to talk, Dr. Waterstone."

She knew the voice. Her heart sank. "Major Smith! Whatever this is, give it up. You don't known how dangerous…"

"I know exactly how dangerous this is. That's why I'm here."

Another man stepped behind Dr. Kay. She caught a flash of white lab coat, turned, and saw that the man behind her was tall and slender. His head was bald. Thick lenses on heavy steel frames covered eyes that had no brows.

"Dr. Steiner, meet Dr. Waterstone."

The bald man nodded. He smiled with thin lips.

"I must apologize, Dr. Waterstone." Steiner spoke with a heavy German accent. "I'm sorry we had you bound, but as you can see, we are all quite busy. We had no one to watch you. And I was not sure you would recover."

Dr. Kay felt Bulldog's foul breath on her neck, felt him lift her hands from her back and cut the bonds around her wrists. Circulation came back into her fingers. She rubbed her hands and swept her eyes across a narrow table that ran underneath the panel of mirrors. Smith's muscular back blocked most of her view. But surgical instruments were in sight. She shuddered.

"What do you want?" Dr. Kay asked.

"I want you to continue your work under my direction."

"That's impossible."

"Nothing's impossible with you, Dr. Waterstone. I know all about you."

"Then you know I won't help you."

"On the contrary, Dr. Waterstone, you will help me." Smith's voice was different, frightening. "I know about you in ways you could not possibly imagine. I've followed your career for a long time."

She felt the strength begin to leave her legs. She locked them.

"This project of yours exceeds my wildest dreams." Smith dimmed the lights on his mirrors, took off his aviator glasses, and turned. In the shadows, his eyes were dark holes. "We both like wild dreams, don't we?"

"I don't know what you're talking about."

"Of course you do." His voice was calm, almost hypnotic. "I understand everything about you. You were born in 1963 in Baltimore. Your father was once an academic, the kind he hoped you would be. You graduated from Johns Hopkins at the top of your class at the age of nineteen. And then that business with that young marine. Your father's high hopes crushed in a moment of passion. I understand that the two of you, father and daughter, still rarely speak."

"Shut up."

"A marriage by a justice of the peace in Atlantic City. A farewell to your education. You threw away everything. You were pregnant when your young marine was killed by a terrorist bomb in a third world nation half the globe away. Your father greeted that news with considerable enthusiasm, didn't he?"

"I'm warning you, Smith."

"Yes, I believe you are warning me. Your penchant for hurting those who hurt you is something I admire. After your young marine's death, you raised your child and resumed your education with renewed energy. But not to become a dusty academic! You wanted to hurt them back, didn't you?"

She fought to hold her temper. She clenched her fists.

"Your first patent was a birth control device that you tested in the third world. Can't have the wrong sort reproducing, can we? Not the unhappy third world kind with offspring who grow up and throw bombs."

"You're wrong. What I did was to prevent starvation, poverty, unhappiness, the kind that produces violence and revolutions and starving babies with swollen bellies. It was safe and…"

"Spare me the idealism." Smith interrupted. "Your next patent was on an anti-toxin that could have been cheaply produced and used to save lives in the same starving countries. That distribution never took place."

"The company's decision. Not mine. After that, I left because…"

"Because your work brought you to the attention of the Pentagon. You agreed with them that biologics and chemicals would be the poor man's nuclear weapon, that they would be the perfect tool for third world dictators. You went to work willingly."

"To make the world safer."

"For revenge against the same third world that took your husband."

"If you think that, you know nothing about me. You lousy, perverted…" She stopped herself, reminded herself that Smith had control of Bell Tower, that Mop Up had not been initiated.

"Don't take offense, Dr. Waterstone. I'm all for revenge." Smith's face remained motionless, as if his muscles were frozen. "And I admire your dedication. No time for anything but your work. No time for your daughter."

Dr. Kay fought to control her anger.

"No time for your daughter and no time for men. Except one. And even that one man you've kept on your terms, haven't you?"

"You're a sick bastard!"

Smith clicked on his surgical lamps. His eyes were dull, brown, empty. Underneath his eyes, there were thick surgical scars. His eyelids seemed wrong, never blinked. Sometime in the past, Smith must have had severed facial injuries or maybe botched plastic surgery. Smith perceived that she was studying him. He spoke. "After the injuries and after the men who called themselves doctors finished their work, I was unable to sleep with my eyes closed, unable to blink away dust or harsh light. But that wasn't the worst, eh Steiner?"

"No, it was not the worst." Steiner answered.

Smith turned and bent over his table, pulled contact lenses from his eyes. Dr. Kay watched the mirror. The brown eyes were gone. Violet eyes cast their reflection in the mirror. They were penetrating and cruel.

"Who are you?" she asked.

"You don't recognize me? I'm truly disappointed."

Smith lowered his face over a bowl and let Steiner rinse his head with a water jet. Brown die filled the bowl, leaving Smith's skull capped in fine white hair. There were more scars under the hair. Dr. Kay noticed syringes and vials. Smith didn't touch them.

"The scars, I can hide with injections. But the effect is short." Smith's hands moved toward his flaccid face. "I can wear my appliances for only a few hours at a time. An ordinary man might consider them too painful to wear at all. But I am not an ordinary man." Smith reached inside his mouth and removed the steel medical devices. "Without these, I have nothing but crushed bones." He stood and turned.

His face was hideous.

It was a face that was logged in the computers of over a hundred police and intelligence departments. Some flattered him with a title, labeled him a weapons scientist. Others labeled him with a list of crimes. It was a long list. His was the face of a madman, powerful around the eyes and forehead and formless beneath. He looked like a living skeleton.

"Rykoff!" Dr. Kay felt her insides turn cold. "I thought you were dead."

"In my former country, this is the reward for ambition." He touched his face. "But I'm hard to kill."

"You're nothing but a damn arms merchant." Her words came out by themselves. She surprised herself.

"Weapons technology is a science in any age." He moved in close. His eyes were burning. "I'm going to blend my science with yours."

"I won't help you turn Bell Tower into a weapon." She tried to back up. There was no place to move.

"I'm certain you'll reconsider." Rykoff spoke calmly. He nodded to Bulldog, who held up a hand radio.

"Downsize." Bulldog spoke into his radio.

The automatic weapons fire came from the distance. It blended with screams. It seemed to go on forever. Or maybe it was the silence that followed that seemed to go on forever.

"What have you done?" She knew the answer. Jennings and the others were dead.

"No one ever refuses me." Rykoff whispered.

Dr. Kay looked at Viktor Rykoff and knew what she had to do. He had control of Bell Tower, and there was no way for her to signal for Mop Up. Maybe Washington would take independent action and initiate Mop Up. Maybe not. But there was still the reality that Rykoff had kept her alive because she was essential to his plan. And maybe, without her, his work would never get done. She knew what she had to do. Make him mad enough to lose control. Hopefully it would end with a bullet to her head. Hopefully there would be no pain.

"A face like yours?" She said it loud. "I'm sure you've been refused a lot."

He remained almost placid. He even seemed amused.

"You can't get this job done without me. And I won't help you."

Rykoff reached into the darkness under his panel of mirrors. He came up with a green duffel bag. She recognized it and felt every muscle in her body tense with anger and fear. Once the duffel bag had belonged to her husband. She'd kept it, traveled with it.

"You're very brave, aren't you?" Rykoff's voice was almost robotic. He reached into the bag and removed a picture frame. The photograph was Dr. Kay's favorite, taken of her and April in Chesapeake the previous summer. April had even let Dr. Kay put her arms around her.

"I wonder, dear Doctor Waterstone. Does bravery run in your family?"

"You leave her alone, Rykoff. You hear me? You leave her alone!"

Rykoff didn't listen. His eyes were on the photo.

Chapter Eight

The Federal Express van arrived hours after dark and parked at a bend in the road. In the driver's seat, a big man with a pockmarked face used gloved hands to wipe condensation from the windows. The muscular woman in the passenger seat did the same and told the big man that she had a good view of the Waterstone house.

The house was sheltered from the neighbors by dense pines. The street lights were sparse. The inside lights were on in only two places, one window upstairs and one down. Across the upstairs one, there were two shadows. Downstairs there was only one. All in all, three people inside the house.

It was cold and drizzling, a bad night for a walk. Neighbors would likely stay at home. In the front seat of the van, the man and woman agreed it was perfect.

The woman liked to call herself Jack. Her Federal Express uniform was meant for a stocky man, but it fit her muscled body perfectly. A guard at Down State Women's Correctional Facility had provided the injections to build that body. The same guard had seen to it that Jack had gotten a job in the infirmary and access to sedative drugs that limited the ability of her cell mates to defend themselves. In turn, Jack had done whatever was asked of her, mostly making sure that selected inmates kept certain guards happy. Jack had enjoyed it, especially the rough stuff. And the guards had been appreciative. Just before Jack had made parole, a guard put her on to an outside job.

"Getting late." Jack opened her side window, raised a parabolic sound amplifier, and pointed it at the second floor. She slipped a plug earphone in place.

The big, pockmarked man behind the wheel said nothing. He knew it was best for him if he said very little.

"Who put you on to this job?" Jack removed the earphone.

"Same people who put you on to it." The big man lied, same as when he'd told the woman his name was Spud. No reason to tell her the truth. With your accomplices, truth was a bad thing. Your accomplices always turned you in.

"When?" Jack asked.

"Month ago." This time, Spud told the truth. "Told me to be ready. Said if the job wasn't needed, I could keep the down payment. This afternoon I got the call that the job was on." He didn't tell Jack that he'd already been to the fancy prep school and watched the target.

"Yeah. Same as me." Jack seemed satisfied. She put her earphone back in place.

Spud avoided small talk. Things always slipped when you got into small talk on a job. Police work had taught him the rules. If you can, do it alone. Always keep your mouth shut. Of course, he was no longer a policeman, a career ended by his bad temper and what he'd done to a suspect in his custody at the city jail. Restraints hadn't kept the suspect from pissing Spud off. The suspect had ended up dead. Spud's partner had sobered up long enough feel bad about what Spud had done, sobered up long enough to talk to the DA, but not to the grand jury. Spud had been lucky, ended up with forced retirement instead of charges.

"Got something." Jack clicked on the single speaker on the seat.

The two voices on the speaker were female. A male voice joined them. It was garbled. It was traveling by phone.

"Won't be much longer now." Jack smiled.

Spud shrugged. He retrieved the photograph he'd taken to the school. He studied it under the glow of his Zippo lighter. The Waterstone girl was pretty, damn pretty. He said so.

"Yeah, this is going to be fun." Jack agreed.

"You're not getting paid to have fun." Spud clicked the Zippo closed. "You do not want to screw around with the people you're working for. Not these people. Got that?"

"I got it." Jack pulled out her earphone. She looked at April Waterstone's photograph. "It's still going to be fun."

***

In the second floor bedroom on the east end of the house, April Waterstone rolled to her stomach on her bed and made room for her new girlfriend, Heather Skone, to share the ear piece of her telephone. Heather was clumsy, damn clumsy. Worse, she giggled near the phone. April swiped at her.

"You sure you're alone?" Stagmire was on the other end. He was loud.

"Damn right, I'm alone. Why wouldn't I be?" April found herself rocking her legs. She crossed her ankles to make them stop.

"I thought I heard someone else."

"Not here. Maybe you've got someone."

"Nah," he hesitated. "What are you wearing?"

"You know what I'm wearing."

"Tell me anyway."

"I'm wearing your football jersey."

"And what else?"

"And boxer shorts."

"And what else?"

"That's all."

"Sounds comfortable. Maybe I should come over."

"No."

"Why?"

"Because it's a school night." April rolled her eyes.

"You're smart, Waterstone. A school night shouldn't matter." Stagmire laughed into the phone. "Give me another reason. A good reason."

"Because I said so, Stagmire. That good enough?" April rolled on her back and twisted the phone cord of the land line she hardly ever used.

"We still have a date, Saturday night."

"That's right." April softened her voice.

"What if I can't wait?"

"You'll have to, Stagmire." April made eye contact with Heather. "Dottie's in charge, which means we can stay out late. Bye." She hung up the phone before Stagmire could.

"Cool." Heather said.

April sat up and went back to painting her nails. She did it like she was angry. "He's an airhead."

"He's real cute."

"He's a lousy kisser. All open mouth and tongue coming at you before he even gets there. I get saliva all over my chin."

"That's not his rep."

"His rep's wrong." April didn't look up from her work. "Trust me. He'd rather be drinking beer with his buddies and looking for fights. He never finds fights, thank God. Just talks about them, drunk on our land line at midnight. You can hear the other guys in the background, egging him on. He wants to come over."

"Does he?"

"What do you think?" April started to say more, but the phone rang again. She let it keep ringing.

"Aren't you going to answer it?" Heather stared at April.

"No." April kept painting her nails. "It's Wednesday. It's eight o'clock. It's Tech."

"Jeez, Waterstone." Heather laughed. "You mad at the world or what?"

"Not the world."

April was right about H.I. Tech. He did call her every Wednesday night. That night, Heather watched April do what she always did, rewind the machine and erase the message without listening.

"Cool!" Heather put on her shoes, grabbed her books, and started to leave.

"Where're you going?"

"Home. I didn't realize it was eight."

***

Inside the parked van, Jack wiped the fogged window with her gloved hand and compared the young girl leaving the Waterstone house with the one in the photo. The one in the photo was pretty, real pretty. Not so the one climbing into the red Wrangler in the driveway. Must be a girlfriend. Jack watched her drive away. "One down. Two to go."

"This one's mine." Spud turned on a laptop computer and found the program he wanted. The program would interact with any phone, writing the number and name of the DC police on the caller ID. He connected his modem to his cell phone and made sure the microphone on the laptop was working. He keyed in the number to Dottie Sinclair's house.

"Why you calling the Sinclair home?"

"Proper procedure. I'll either pick up a message or get her call forwarding."

A woman answered the phone on the second ring.

"She's got call forwarding." Spud turned and spoke into the laptop microphone. He made his voice sound like gravel. "Is a Mr. Mike Sinclair at home?"

"I'm sorry. He's not. This is his wife, Dottie. Can I help you?"

"Yes, ma'am. This is Sergeant Ruskin with the DC police." Spud used the name of his prior shift sergeant. "Does your husband own a 1995 black, BMW convertible with custom plates, SINC 1?"

"Has something happened to it?"

"Stolen and recovered, ma'am. The two youths were driving a little fast and got pulled over. I'll need you to come downtown and identify it."

"Now?"

"Yes, ma'am." Spud gave her an address in downtown Washington.

Five minutes later, Dottie Sinclair exited the Waterstone house, climbed into Dr. Kay's Suburban, and drove away. Only one light burned in one window of the house. It was upstairs.

"It's your turn." Spud motioned to Jack. She climbed out the van and retrieved a large trunk. Spud opened the glove box and grabbed the wire cutters.

***

Inside the house, April was already asleep atop her bed. She hadn't meant to, but Bagley's math problem had put her out cold. When the doorbell woke her on the fourth ring, she decided to ignore it. It rang a fifth time. She cursed and told herself that if it was Stagmire, she'd cancel Saturday night. She climbed off the bed and padded toward the edge of the stairs. Then she remembered she wasn't really dressed. She peered over the top of the banister and saw the face in the paneled glass of the front door.

For a second, she couldn't decide if it was a woman's or a man's face. She decided it was a woman. She descended the stairs.

The tile floor of the foyer was freezing. April tried to warm her feet on the front Persian rug. It slid, as she stepped on to it, almost making her lose her balance. Beyond the fogged glass, she could see the woman's broad, leathery face and a fur hat with some sort of postal badge. Damn ugly woman was April's first thought. Then she felt a tinge of regret for calling her ugly. April placed the chain lock and opened the door a crack.

"Federal Express. Delivery for Dr. Waterstone." The woman's breath steamed into the cold air. She looked at April warmly.

"She's out of the country."

"That's okay, dear. You can sign for it. Or I can leave you a card and someone can pick it up later." The woman's eyes were glowing.

April saw the large metal trunk sitting on the porch. The Federal Express woman was alone. The woman smiled at her in an almost motherly way.

"It's okay. I'll sign for it."

April unlocked the chain and opened the door. The chill made her wrap her arms about her shoulders. The Federal Express woman lifted the trunk with one arm and carried it inside.

"Not very heavy, is it?"

"No dear. It's not."

Shivering, April pushed the door closed. It struck something in mid-swing and came back at her. She turned and tried to register what she was seeing.

The big man came from nowhere, forcing himself inside. He had a pockmarked face and had the collar on his dirty overcoat turned up. But that wasn't where April's mind focused. It was on his hands. Big hands in surgical gloves. They were reaching for her, even as he kicked the door closed behind him.

Run! Her mind screamed at her.

April slammed into the woman in the uniform. Beside the woman, the trunk was open and empty except for a restraining strap and a blanket. April hesitated a critical second, her mind still trying to register what was happening. The big man grabbed her arms. The syringe came from nowhere. The woman held it.

"There are two ways to do this, girl." The woman's voice changed. It was mean. "The hard way or the easy way. I'd love it if you made it the hard way."

"I warned you, Jack," the man momentarily loosened his grip. I told…"

April bashed the man's face with the back of her head. She felt his chin rebound and heard his lip split. In the same instant, she jammed her bare heal into the toe of his shoe, felt him gasp and let go. She hurled herself forward.

"You go, girl!" The woman was smiling.

April side-stepped the woman and bolted into the dark living room, knocking over a chair. She slammed through the dining room and into the kitchen. At the back door, the alarm keypad showed a green, inactive light. April punched in the panic number.

The lights and alarms blasted in her ears.

April wrenched open the back door and started into the cold. She never made it. The hands that wrenched her back into the house felt like steel. They were hairy hands that hiked up the sleeves of a postal uniform as they moved across April's chest and crushed her. April felt a shaved face press close against her cheek. April tried to kick, striking air twice, before the pock-faced man grabbed her ankles.

"The alarm! The police will be here any…" April didn't finish. The woman shoved a hand across her mouth.

"No they won't, girl." The woman kissed April's cheek with lips like leather.

The man showed April the wire cutters. "You're not connected to the alarm company. Your neighbors aren't coming either. So don't give Jack a reason to make this tougher than it has to be."

"Tell me the code or I'll break your arm." Jack tightened a grip that already felt like steel.

"No."

Jack twisted April's arm, as if it were made of rubber. The pain shot into April's shoulder, and she felt as if she would throw up. She blurted out the deactivation code, 2001, her high school graduation year.

The big man punched in the code. The alarm stopped.

April let herself go limp. Jack hauled her back into the foyer. At the trunk, the man locked April's ankles between his own, before she had a chance to kick. The woman spoke first. "This time, Spud. Hold her tight."

"Shut up, Jack. Don't piss me off." Spud slid his arm under April's chin and locked her neck in the crook. He reminded himself not to squeeze too hard. That had been how he'd killed the inmate, squeezing too hard.

April felt Spud relax his grip. She lurched against him, almost getting clear. The big man squeezed her neck, compressing her windpipe. April felt herself getting dizzy. Her vision was going black. She let her body relax. She struggled to talk. It came out as a whisper. "It's okay. I won't fight."

Spud relaxed his grip. April got her wind back. She saw Jack raise a syringe in one hand, an alcohol pad in the other.

"Don't!" April heard the pleading in her own voice. "Who are you? Why are you doing this?"

"Don't you need a tourniquet?" Spud asked Jack.

"Nah! This stuff works fast right in the muscle. It'll keep her out for about forty-five minutes."

"All the way to the airport."

"Yeah, but she may wake up with some real bad dreams and thrashing."

"Not our problem. They can deal with that on the plane."

April felt the panic rising. She kicked one leg free. The big man tightened his grip around her neck, and her vision faded again. She winced as Jack jabbed the needle into her exposed shoulder.

"You don't need that." April spoke wild-eyed. "Please! I'll go quietly."

Jack smiled. "Yes, girl. You will go quietly. Sweet dreams." She moved her thumb to the plunger but froze as the doorbell rang.

"Help…" April tried to scream. Spud slapped his left hand over her mouth and tightened his arm around her neck. Jack removed the needle without injecting.

"There's a kid at the front door." Jack peaked through a crack in the curtain.

"You do exactly what I tell you," Spud whispered into April's ear. He removed his hand from her mouth and shoved her into Jack's grip. He nodded to Jack. She squeezed April by the back of her neck and nudged her toward the door.

Chapter Nine

For H.I. Tech it was the end of a bad day. But bad was far from over. He got home from Dunbar's at seven, still in his sacker's uniform and smelling like brown paper bags and groceries. The phone rang five times before he gave in and answered. On the other end was the familiar female voice that always sounded like a robot.

"Good evening. Answering service for Dr. Hendrick. Calling for Dr. Tech."

"He's not in. Have you tried beeping him?"

"Yes. He hasn't answered."

"Crap!" H.I. said it into the phone. He knew what Doc's not answering his pager meant. There was only one place he could go that was electronically shielded, one place where signals couldn't get to his beeper.

"Crap!" H.I. said it again.

"Beg your pardon." The woman's voice rose an octave, still sounded like a robot.

"I'm sorry. He's not in. Can I give him a message?"

"Yes tell him Dr. Hendrick will take his calls for the next week. Please have him beep Dr. Hendrick when he gets home."

"I'll tell him." H.I. slammed the phone down and swung his fists at an imaginary target. He punched air almost long enough to blow off steam. But blowing off steam wasn't in the cards. So he waited for the inevitable next phone call, the one where Doc would tell him where the two of them were going on another one of Doc's jobs.

The phone did not ring.

H.I. climbed to the observatory, lit the gas space heater, and turned off the lights. He always found it was easier to think in the dark, but at that moment nothing was easy. He turned on the television and punched the remote to the local news.

The news was bad too. The caption under the sound bite read FILE. Larry King was facing a sweating Raymond Marsden. Marsden was taking off his glasses, fumbling with them, wiping them with a handkerchief.

"Are you calling it a UFO?"

"Accepting that *UFO* merely means unidentified, I would have to say yes."

The sound bite was replaced by live coverage. A cold street in DC. Lots of onlookers behind police tape and a uniformed officer with a microphone shoved in his face. They watched as a body under a bloody sheet was loaded into the back of an ambulance.

"Is there any evidence of foul play?"

"There are no signs of a struggle. We do have a note, and at this time our opinion is that this was suicide. Apparently he jumped from the twelfth floor."

A still photo of Marsden filled the screen, captioned with the years of Marsden's birth and death. The image slowly cut to a stone-faced anchor, face full of practiced sadness and stoicism. "Dr. Raymond Marsden was fifty-three."

H.I. turned off the set and sat in dark staring at the orange glow from the space heater on the other side of the room. He thought of Marsden's meteorite or comet, thought of what it meant to reach for something and not get it. Marsden failed in front of the whole world. He'd had nothing left but a long fall, Yale professorship to a lonely DC hotel room to a cold pavement.

The shock faded into disbelief, then to nothing. H.I. sat a long time, ignoring the TV and hating the world. At eight o'clock, he reminded himself it was Wednesday, picked up the phone and dialed April. She didn't answer. That was usual. So was her message machine. No voice, just a long beep and the sound of recording heads. It was pointless leaving a message. He knew he'd never hear back, told himself he was done with her but knew he wasn't.

The observatory phone rang. He let the answering machine take it, listened to his own voice on tape.

"This is 301-984-1730. I'm not home right now. I've probably gotten my butt dragged out of town by Doc again. So leave a message at the sound of the beep, and I'll get back to you one day. If this is Mom, rethink custody." The machine beeped.

"Pick up the phone, H.I." Doc sounded pissed.

"Is this what I think it is?" H.I. cradled the receiver against his ear.

"Pack our bags!"

"Doc! I…"

"Do it quickly. Tropical clothes, bug repellent, medical bag. And stay where you are. McCready is on the way to get you."

H.I. knew what the list meant. They were going someplace no one sane would ever want to vacation. The mention of McCready was worse. He was CIA, not an agent but a security guard. He moonlighted for Doc. Tropical stuff and McCready! Bad news! H.I. told Doc so. "I can't leave now, Doc."

Doc hung up. H.I. carried his books down into his room, pulled a familiar, worn duffel bag from the closet, and started to pack. His books were scattered on the bed. The *Elle* was on top of the biology textbook. The blonde with the naked back was looking at the world with a sultry mouth and bedroom eyes. Below her, Dr. Kay Waterstone was the name on the subscription label.

H.I. phoned April again. The line was busy. He called the operator just to prove to himself that she was leaving the phone off of the hook, deliberately avoiding his calls.

"I'm sorry, sir. There's no conversation on the line. It must be out of order."

"Are you sure?"

"There's no conversation, sir. Would you like to report it?"

"Do I sound like I want to report anything, lady?" He slammed the phone down and finished packing. He threw the books in last, looked at the *Elle* cover for maybe a second, then got the keys to the jeep.

Two minutes later his duffel bag was in the back seat of his jeep, and H.I. was driving downhill on the loop.

The loop was only two lanes wide. On both sides big yards sloped up to rambling ranch homes, most of them dark. The street lights were sparse. But he knew every inch of that street. He'd grown up there. He'd met April there, the day she moved in.

The first time he'd ever seen her, he'd found her trying to kill Alan Brogan with her bicycle. Strong for a girl was what he'd first thought. No that hadn't been his first thought at all. His first thought had been that she was beautiful even when totally pissed. His second thought had been that she was older than him. But his second thought had been wrong. She'd been just a twelve year old kid! But a tough twelve year old kid. She'd sent Brogan running for his life.

Brogan had been strong, but she'd been stronger. He'd tried to use the sloping yards to gain ground and tire her out. But she hadn't tired at all. She'd been all legs scissoring the pedals as if her bike were flying. Brogan had been merely mean. But she'd been seriously pissed off.

"Pick up sticks! Pick up sticks!" Brogan had meant it as an insult, because she'd been thin as a rail and about as long. He'd said it to make her cry and give up. But she'd done neither.

"You're going to die, shit head!" She'd meant it.

She'd shot within only a foot of H.I. as she'd closed on Brogan. For a bare second the two of them had made eye contact, hers liquid blue and H.I.'s lost in them. In that fraction of a moment, he'd sworn he was seeing her anger fade, her sudden smile meeting his briefly. Then she'd continued bearing down on Brogan, blonde hair flying above her Guns N Roses T-shirt. She'd knocked Brogan on to his back, pinned him down, and slapped the hell out of him. Brogan had cried. She hadn't.

Later H.I. had learned who she was, that she'd moved from Virginia, and that she was living with her mom four blocks away. By then, all of Brogan's friends were calling her sticks and hoping to torment her. By then the girls were giving her a bad time too. It was the guys' way of flirting, Doc had explained. Meant they liked her. And it was the girls' being jealous of her looks. They'd grow out of it. Put it all together, and it was just the basic psychology of growing up. It was nothing more, Doc had said. But for H.I. it had been very much more.

"You believe in love at first sight?" he'd asked Doc.

"You're too damn young to be in love."

"Answer the question, Doc."

"First sight is a bad idea," he'd answered. He and H.I.'s mom were separating for the final time, thinking they would do better as friends. She'd maintained that she really wanted a quieter life than the one she had with Doc. She'd said she'd be moving to New York City.

"You meet some cute girl?"

"No. Just asking." H.I had lied but Doc had seen right through him.

"At your age, you'll be over it in a week."

"Sure, Doc."

For two years after that, H.I. had had April Waterstone mostly to himself. He'd been nice to her when others had not. So the two of them would go to movies, watch TV, rid bikes, and go swimming. All kid stuff. All fun. And always warm in a way nothing had ever been warm before. He'd wanted it to go on forever. But that was not to be.

April Waterstone would develop early. Where she had once been sticks she would become willowy and curved.

For a time she would be taller than H.I. Older guys would notice. Brogan and his friends would notice too, and they'd make up stories. They'd call her a tease. Girls would call her worse. So she'd hang with him and tune the rest of them out. He'd love having her all to himself. Love it until the day when he'd be the one to hurt her. His doing. His fault. It still haunted him.

On the loop, H.I. stepped harder on the gas. The clock on the dashboard read eight fifteen. By now McCready was probably already at his house and looking for him. Maybe he was already calling Doc on a cell phone to tell him that his son and the jeep were gone. Doc would be pissed. No big deal. At least then they'd be on even ground, both pissed speechless all the way to wherever Doc was hauling him. That'd be fine with H.I. Maybe Doc would be mad enough to let him stay home this time. That would be a good thing. But H.I. doubted things would turn out good.

He hit the gas and checked himself in the rearview mirror. His parka was unzipped and open across his sacker's uniform. A fricking sacker's uniform! He ripped away the bow tie. It was all he could do. No time to go back and change. If he did, he'd run into McCready, who was probably already waiting.

H.I. opened his collar, slammed the wheel, and stepped harder on the gas. Light from street lamps came and went, flickering on the *Elle* magazine making the sultry blonde look like a cheap, silent film. He nudged the jeep downhill on the loop, swung four blocks around the curve, and gunned uphill on April's street.

He almost hit the Federal Express van, before he saw it. It was waiting in the crook of the last curve. He hit the brakes and slid around it. The van was driverless and unlit with its tail pipe spewing exhaust in the dark. Something was screwy. That was all H.I. told himself. He didn't give it a second thought. His mind was elsewhere. What he was going to say to April was going to really piss her off. That was better than the other reaction he might get. The other reaction was that she might not give a damn.

He parked at the street and walked. Her driveway was empty. The Suburban was gone. The house was dark everywhere except for her room upstairs and the foyer downstairs. Magazine under his arm, H.I. made his way to the porch. He thought about the exact words he was going to use. He straightened himself up and checked his appearance in his reflection in the glass panels beside the front door. What he saw wasn't good. He was a tall and lanky kid wearing the uniform of a grocery clerk. He was all arms and legs and had dark, angular looks begging for a shave. Looks like this weren't going to win the argument he was about to have with the love of his life.

His first doorbell ring brought her face to the glass. She was upset. He'd expected upset. She was never glad to see him. She stared at him as if she didn't know what to do. He raised the magazine. She opened the door a crack.

She was naked except for a football jersey. No, not naked! He saw the bottoms of school boxer shorts peaking underneath the jersey. The jersey itself hung loosely around her throat. She covered her breasts with folded arms.

"I can't talk, Tech. What do you want?" She sounded mad, but she looked scared. She glanced out of the side of her eyes and then back at him. H.I. realized that it wasn't fear in those blue eyes. It was terror. Her eyes were wide and darting. "What do you want, Tech?"

"Where's Dottie?"

"Not here." She glanced out of the side of her eyes again. She was trembling. "I can't talk. What do you want?"

Suddenly it was all clear to him. As far as he knew, April Waterstone had never done it with any guy. But as he stood on that porch and watched her fidget, it became clear that she was finally maybe doing it with some guy while Dottie was away. The possibility hurt like an acetylene torch in H.I.'s chest.

"Who's in there, April?"

"Nobody. Just me."

"Is it Stagmire?"

"God, no! I promise to God, Tech! If you spread anything like that at school, I'll…" She cut herself off. She was almost crying.

"Are you okay, April?"

"Yeah. I'm okay. Tell me what you want. I have to go."

"You dropped this magazine." He held up the *Elle*.

She said nothing. She just stared at him.

"Right, April. I'm damn glad to see you too. Have a real nice life!"

He stuffed the magazine back under his arm and turned around. He was walking away for the last time. He thought about where he was going: first a car ride with McCready and then a long plane ride with Doc. It was a bad night getting worse, the story of his life. Before he reached the first step, April was out the door and grabbing at his arm.

"I'm sorry. That was sweet of you." She slipped an arm around his waist, almost pushing the two of them off the porch. "I'll just walk you to your car."

"That's a real bad idea, kid." The man who said it was suddenly standing in the doorway.

He was big and balding with a thin, pockmarked face and a cruel mouth. H.I. recognized him immediately as the cop he'd seen at school. Instinctively, H.I. froze in place. April grasped his arm tighter and retreated behind his back. H.I.'s mind reeled, trying to grasp what was happening.

The cop had been at Adams Day, because he'd been looking for April. He'd followed Stagmire off campus only because Stagmire had been driving April. This was all about April! But why? H.I. tried to think of an answer while coming up with something to say to the cop. But things were happening too fast.

The cop was raising something in his hand. H.I. expected to see a badge, but he was wrong. What he saw was a long black cylinder. It looked heavy. A nightstick maybe? Or didn't cops call it a baton? But the cop wasn't holding it like he'd seen cops hold nightsticks. The cop was raising it in a controlled arc as he grasped the far end in a pistol grip with his hand protected by a surgical glove. It was only then that H.I. realized the long cylinder was a silencer attached to an automatic pistol.

And then was entirely too late.

Chapter Ten

At eight fifteen, McCready was four blocks from April's house and breaking into H.I. Tech's backyard. By law he shouldn't have been there. Neither should Hitchcock, the man McCready had with him. After all, they were both CIA.

The CIA seal is circular and mostly red, white, and blue. On its face the American bald eagle's head rests upon a shield embossed with a rose compass with sixteen points. By law the CIA can spy on everyone but American citizens. The investigation of American citizens falls under the umbrella of the FBI and only takes place if a federal crime is suspected. There are other intelligence agencies besides the CIA and FBI, and in a perfect world, they'd all share information and coordinate. In the real world they have interagency rivalry, and the boat gets missed sometimes.

Mostly the CIA is supposed to gather intelligence, so America doesn't have any more Pearl Harbors or Iran hostage crises. Sometimes the CIA does more than gather information. Sometimes it engages in covert action, the dagger part of cloak and dagger. By law the CIA has to have the approval of the president to use its dagger. But as in any organization, not everyone follows the rules.

So McCready and Hitchcock should not have been anywhere near the Tech home. And what they were doing was in truth a felony.

Of the two men in the Tech yard, Hitchcock should have known better. He wasn't a security guard like McCready. Hitchcock was in the clandestine service. Being a member of the clandestine service was supposed to make him cautious, but Hitchcock was in too big a hurry to be cautious. He was only along with McCready because he'd been asked at the last minute. Hitchcock was supposed to be taking a rest after a whole year in Saudi Arabia. He'd damn-well earned that rest and planned to spend it with a secretary he'd met at Langley. She'd seemed eager, too eager for Hitchcock to be off riding around with McCready and picking up some kid in Bethesda. But here in Bethesda he was. Ramsey had asked him. Payback time, Ramsey had called it. Think of it as a favor returned, Ramsey had added. Hitchcock was determined that the favor be a quick one, but it wasn't turning out that way.

"What do you mean the little bastard's not home?" Hitchcock said.

"I mean the kid's not home." McCready shrugged it off. McCready worked as a security protective officer at the complex in Langley, spent boring shifts wearing a guard's uniform and walking a beat. For McCready acting as H.I. Tech's chauffeur was a way to supplement his low-pay position. He did it all the time. This time Ramsey had asked McCready to take Hitchcock along to pick H.I. up, but he hadn't said why. McCready didn't care. Hitchcock did.

Hitchcock kicked open the side gate and walked around the back of the Tech house. By instinct, he moved like a cat, stayed in the shadows, and made no noise. McCready shrugged and followed him, swept his eyes over the story-and-a-half and saw that everything was dark. McCready shrugged again. Hitchcock kicked over a lawn chair and cursed.

"He really is gone."

"The Tech kid does this all the time," McCready said. "He'll be along after a while."

"I'm not fricking waiting." Hitchcock checked his watch. "Shit!"

"I'm telling you not to blow a fuse, Hitchcock. The kid will be back on his own."

Hitchcock told himself he wasn't waiting. He walked back to the driveway, opened the passenger door, and climbed into McCready's battered, white Plymouth. As McCready climbed behind the wheel, his parka opened. The interior light fell on the handle of the .357 magnum that McCready wore in holster.

"What, McCready? You're packing?"

"Never leave home without it. I don't plan to be a statistic."

Hitchcock shook his head. He was not armed. He looked at the dark house and his watch, saw that it was seventeen after eight. He'd have to make up some really lame excuse for being late. Otherwise the woman would just assume he didn't care, might even tell him to forget the whole thing. Hitchcock promised himself that he wasn't going to let that happen, not after a year in Saudi. He pulled his cell phone out of his jacket.

"What are you doing, Hitchcock?"

"Calling in a favor. I got one called on me. Now it's my turn."

Hitchcock's digital phone had been given to him when he'd left Langley two hours earlier. The phone was fitted with scrambler. He punched in the familiar number, let the machine on the other end answer, and punched in the extension for O.I.T., Office of Information Technology. The machine voice asked for his pass code. He punched it in on his phone.

"O.I.T. This is Nordman." A human voice answered.

"This is Hitchcock."

"Are you secure?"

"I am secure."

"What do you want, Hitchcock?"

"Help. The fast and personal kind. I want you to phone Fort Meade."

"The NSA? Are you nuts?"

The National Security Agency is as big as the CIA, but its mission is to monitor communications from around the world. Its computers can scan millions of telephones at one time and retrieve information instantly.

"Your buddy in Meade owes you a favor, Nordman. You owe me." Hitchcock told Nordman he wanted the telephone numbers and corresponding addresses of all calls that had come through the two lines at the Tech home in the preceding two hours. He especially wanted the traffic from the Tech kid's home phone.

"Tell you what, Hitchcock. I'm on break in thirty minutes. I'll do it then."

Hitchcock looked at his watch, saw it was eight eighteen. "You owe me big time, Nordman. You'll do it now."

Chapter Eleven

"Both of you step back into the house." The big man clicked off the safety on his silenced automatic. To H.I., the mouth of the silencer looked like a cannon.

In the light he could see the pistol was a model 1911 .45 caliber, the grandfather of all automatic pistol designs and still being manufactured after eighty-eight years. H.I. had fired one with Doc on the gun range. To fire it a shooter had to rack the slide in order to chamber the first round. The same move also cocked the hammer. A shooter then had to thumb the side safety to release the lock on the hammer. Last he had to squeeze the handle to release the grip safety. Three safeties! As shooters went, the big man was good for two.

"Don't screw around with me, kid." The big man meant it. The pistol he was holding had been developed to fire a bullet big enough and mean enough to knock its target down every time.

H.I.'s mind raced. Rule number one in a confrontation, actually Doc's rule number one, was to appear to cooperate while looking for a crowd and lights and people who might call the police. April's neighbors were hidden by dense pines. Across the street and just beyond the bars of an eight-foot, wrought iron fence, there was a For Sale sign fronting two acres of dark trees and a darker house.

Rule number one was a total bust.

"Do it now!" The big man tightened his grip on his weapon. He was now three for three and ready to shoot.

H.I. felt April squeeze against his back. Any other time he would have liked that a lot, but under the circumstances he barely noticed. He was sweating like crazy. She trailed him into the doorway.

"You were supposed to make him leave." The big man's voice was a mean whisper.

"I tried to." April retreated against H.I.

"You messed up. Now it's your friend's problem." The big man pointed his pistol directly into H.I.'s face.

There were a lot of questions H.I. wanted to ask. His mind worked like that, even when it was a bad time to ask questions. Like what the hell was going on? Like where was Stagmire? Like where was Dottie, and how long had the big guy been at April's house? Yeah, lots of questions cluttered his mind. But he knew he wouldn't ask them. Instead he said something he had no damn intention of doing.

"I can leave now."

"Shut up!" Without changing his aim, the big man spoke over his shoulder. "Hey, Jack, got enough ketamine for two?"

"Nah, just for one." The woman in the Federal Express uniform had a voice deeper than the big man's. The foyer light fell across her lantern jaw and shaved areas around her mouth. She stepped closer, and the same light reflected off a syringe full of clear liquid. Her eyes narrowed to slits focused on April.

"You look like you got plenty of it left." The big man glanced quickly.

"That's because I didn't give her any before the kid rang the doorbell."

Behind the woman a large trunk was open and standing on edge. Inside there was a blanket and a restraining harness. It was for April. They hadn't planned on anyone else.

"No problem." The big man looked right at H.I. "You're not coming along, kid."

"I know that." H.I. swallowed and thought hard about Doc's rule number two The big man kept the silenced pistol raised and stepped backward onto the Persian rug. It slid a little on the cold tile floor. A smile spread across his pockmarked face. "Close the door, kid."

H.I. knew better than to close the door. You never cut off your exit. Doc's rule number two hinged on the presence of an exit. And even then, rule number two was to be used only when your life was threatened. It called for you to create confusion. Confusion was your friend. You were supposed to create it faster than your opponent could think.

H.I. dropped April's *Elle* to the tile floor and stooped to get it. The big man lowered the pistol toward his head. "Don't piss me off, kid."

April moved back a step. The man lost his smile. Now he had to make a decision between two targets in a lighted open doorway that might be seen any moment from a passing car or even a passing constable. The big man made his decision. He raised his pistol until it was pointed halfway between April and H.I. "Girl, you close the door. And you, kid! You stand up."

H.I. held the magazine in a firm grip in his left hand, pointing the pouty blonde's naked back and upper buttocks toward the big man's eyes. Magicians knew this trick. That's why their assistants were always beautiful and half-naked. Great way to distract an audience and hide a move. Great to hide what H.I had in mind, but the big man didn't go for it.

"You think I'm screwing with you? Stand the hell up now."

H.I. followed the order, jerking upward with all the force in his back and long legs. Long legs were good for leverage. And H.I.'s back was powerful. Under the magazine, he held the Persian rug in a death grip in his right hand. He pulled damn hard. The big man's legs left the floor. He fired as he fell.

In the movies a silenced gunshot sounds like a bottle cap popping or maybe a muffled cough. But in that second H.I. found out that movies were bullshit. The silenced gunshot sounded like a dictionary dropped to a tile floor from the ceiling. Its report was a loud crack that echoed off the wall. The bullet's impact was softer, splitting the solid oak door a microsecond before the big man crashed on the tile. A few feet away, the woman dropped her syringe and lunged toward H.I. He caught a glimpse of powerful hands covered in course hair.

Part of rule number two is a reminder. Darkness is your friend. The light switches for the foyer and porch were only inches from H.I.'s right hand. He clicked them just ahead of two sharp cracks from two more silenced shots.

Flashes lit the dark as the bullets slammed into something soft. The flashes lit the woman up like a silent movie as they caught her leaping between H.I. and the big man. She stopped two feet from H.I., hairy hands around her own bleeding throat. She'd taken at least one hit through the carotid artery. H.I. didn't see her hit the floor. He heard it. Then he heard her gurgling blood in her windpipe.

Doc's most important rule was number three. If you couldn't remember any other rule, you could still get by with number three. H.I. yelled it at April.

"Run!"

She was ahead of him instantly, sprinting out the door and running half-naked and barefooted on the freezing ground. He ran behind her, gauging his jeep to be twenty-five feet from the porch. He shoved her past it on purpose. It was locked and the big man did not have a key. The Federal Express van was parked with its engine running and lights off two hundred feet away, probably left that way so as to be ready for a prompt exit after the abuction without attracting attention during it. The van was the obvious choice, a way to leave the big man without a vehicle.

There probably is no rule number four. But if there were, it would be a warning never to look back. H.I. broke it and caught site of the big man bolting over the woman he'd accidentally shot. On the porch he took aim. His first shot was into his partner. He didn't plan on leaving her as a witness. He adjusted his stance and fired again.

Something hot singed the side of H.I.'s left ear and pinged against the wrought iron fence across the street. A second shot popped a hole in the front window of the Federal Express van.

"Keep low."

April slipped out of sight around the driver's side of the Federal Express truck. H.I. heard her scream just before he got to the front grill. He found her pulling at the door and cursing.

"Son-of-a-bitch! Damn thing's locked."

H.I. peered around the hood. The big man was halfway across the yard and walking slowly, silenced automatic in his right hand. He held something else in his left hand. H.I. realized the something else had to be a second set of keys to the van.

"Do something!" April yelled.

The driver's window was almost six feet off the ground. The window mechanism was locked. H.I.'s eyes adjusted to the darkness and made out a rectangular form on the passenger seat. A Mac-10 machine pistol, a drug dealer's favorite. A Mac-10 could empty its twenty round clip in two seconds. All you had to do was point in a general direction at close range and squeeze the trigger. April didn't know a Mac-10 from any other gun. She just knew it was a weapon.

"Break the window," April shouted.

"With what?"

"Your fist!"

"Bullshit!" H.I. grabbed April's hand, spun her in the direction he wanted, and bolted across the street. He kept the two of them low and the van between themselves and the big man. Across the street and beyond the wrought iron fence, there were two acres of dark yard that H.I. knew like the back of his hand. But the fence was slippery, cold, and eight feet high. Impossible to climb.

"Run!"

A shallow drainage ditch fronted the dense pines on April's side of the street. Beyond the pines, a thirty-foot drop ended in a drainage ravine. The far side of the ravine was bordered by narrow, dark woods. Dark was good. Steep was bad. H.I. nixed the thought of using it.

"We run to the loop," he shouted. "We flag a car."

He pulled April downhill. A hundred feet behind, he heard things happen. The van door opened and slammed shut. The engine roared into gear, and the van screeched across the street, jumped the curve, and slammed into the fence. It gunned backward, burning rubber in a fishtail spin. H.I. looked back. That was a bad thing. He looked into blinding lights and a dark windshield, bearing down at high speed.

A cigarette flicked out of the driver's side window and trailed cinders into the dark. Then something bulky was thrust into the same space and pointed ahead. It was the Mac-10, H.I. realized. The van closed the distance between them. H.I. turned his head to run and was surprised to see a second set of headlights.

The second set of headlights was lower to the ground. They flicked on bright and hit H.I. directly in the eyes. Behind them, the engine was smaller than the van's. H.I. blinked and saw the vehicle shoot under a street light, accelerating toward April and him. The vehicle was a battered white Plymouth he knew only too well.

"McCready!" He yelled. "McCready!"

"Get down!" McCready yelled back. The Plymouth veered to the right, squealed on its brakes, and jumped one wheel up on the curb. Driver's window down, McCready waved a pistol in his left hand. In the passenger seat, another man was yelling into a cell phone.

H.I. pulled April hard across the approaching Plymouth's taillights and into the ditch along the roadside. He fell to his chin in freezing, muddy water. April splashed in next to him yelling something in four letters a split second ahead of the gunfire.

McCready's .357 magnum rounds were sharp cracks. The big man's 9mm Mac-10 answered like a row of ear-shattering firecrackers as it emptied a twenty-round clip into McCready's Plymouth. Glass and metal cracked. Some bullets went through the car and whistled through branches. Others ricocheted into the concrete and mixed with the pings of the ejecting shell casings.

H.I.s mind slipped back to the old black-and-white westerns he'd watch with Jefferson Parrish on local television at three o'clock in the morning. The cavalry always seemed to get there in time and save the day. But real life didn't work out that way.

The glass on McCready's Plymouth shattered. The car swerved off the street and slammed into a tree with enough force to throw the rear end off the ground and smash the radiator. Steam rose out of the buckled hood, and the broken horn droned on without stopping. No one got out of the Plymouth.

April peered out of the ditch, then stood soaked and trembling, too exhausted and too numb to run any further. H.I. stood and peeled off his wet parka, feeling the chill all the way to his bones. Downhill, the loop was a hundred yards away. It might as well have been a mile.

"He's stopped." April looked in the direction of the Federal Express van.

The van was idling in the middle of the street and angled toward the wrecked Plymouth. The van's driver's side head-light was busted out. H.I. held his breath and waited for the van to move. It didn't. He lied to himself, told himself the big man was wounded or dead.

"It's over." April didn't seem to feel the mud on her face or know that she was soaked to the skin. H.I. remembered that adrenaline did that kind of stuff to you. It was doing that to him too. It changed what he did and did not notice. Any other time he would have noticed how April's wet jersey stuck to her.

"I think he's dead," she said.

"Keep moving!"

She ran faster than he did, tangled blonde hair falling down the back of her soaked jersey, bare feet padding the cement. He kept up, but got out of breath fast and felt his ribs burning. On the left, April reached a yard that sloped up to an old Tudor. The Tudor was dark except for the porch lights. Across the street, a ranch-style house was dark except for driveway lights. Five hundred feet behind, the van raced its engine. It accelerated downhill, lumbering with a single headlight.

"Shit! He's still after us." H.I. pointed April up the slop-ing yard that led to the Tudor. "Go!"

The wet lawn sank underfoot as H.I. ran upslope behind April. Just ahead of him, she reached the cyclone fence and gate on the left side of the house. H.I. nudged her aside and slammed open the gate. Inside, he could see the entire back yard was built around a swimming pool. Behind the pool, a a garden sloped up to a back fence. H.I. knew that behind the fence there'd be a ledge and a vertical drop of thirty feet into a drainage ravine. Every backyard on this side of the street abutted the same drop.

Behind them the Federal Express van leaped the curb. H.I. spun toward the sound, a 300 horse power V8 engine pushing two and a half tons of machinery out of the dark. It was roaring up the front yard and lighting its way with one working headlight. H.I. grabbed April by the hand and wrenched her through the gate. He shouted what he had in mind.

"Bullshit, Tech. I won't do it."

"No choice!"

Seconds behind them, the van closed the distance. Without dropping his stride, H.I. swept up a brick and smashed the nearest window. The house alarm split the air immediately. It was shrill. It was joined by floodlights blinking from atop the second floor. They lit up the van as it bulldozed over the cyclone gate and fence and became stuck in the wet earth on the side of the house.

April started to buckle. H.I. jerked her upright and pulled her in a run beyond the pool and up the garden slope. The earth was soft, planted with jasmine. The two of them climbed it to the back fence as the van stuck spinning its wheels next to the side of the house. It hung there caught in the floodlights and alarm. H.I. looked down on the scene as he pulled April with him against the fence. He told himself the big man would know the alarm was being relayed. The big man would have to know that in less than a minute the security company would call and get no answer. It would take the security company less than another minute to send the constable who would be within less than yet another minute from the house.

The big man would know time was working against him.
He'd run.

Yeah, right! He'd just shot two Feds. Not likely he'd shake
in his shoes at the prospect of tangling with a rent-a-cop.

H.I. kicked open the back gate and pointed April
through it. Beyond the opening, the floods from the house
blinked into the pitch black hiding a long drop into the
ravine. April froze in place. Behind the two of them, the
van caught traction in the ground. H.I. spun to see it lum-
ber into the back yard, smash lawn furniture, and brake
sideways across the lip of the pool. Then its engine died.
H.I. knew the big man would exit the driver side any second. He'd come for the two of them, and he'd be armed.
H.I. tried again to force April on to the ledge.

"I won't do it, Tech!" April lurched out of his grip.

The van restarted and leaped forward, sending lawn furniture in all directions. It sank in the garden, wheels spinning in mud. H.I. tackled April, flinging the two of them
onto the ledge. The van's wheels gripped the earth, and
the van climbed. The single headlight reflected back from
the fence and illuminated the van's windshield. All bullet
holes and splintered glass! Behind the glass, the big man
held two beefy hands on the wheel. His face was covered in
blood and twisted in rage.

For a millisecond time froze with the big man locking
his eyes on H.I. Then the van hit hard earth at the top of
the sloped garden. The impact spun the van sideways and
slammed it broadside into the fence. Broken boards show-
ered the ledge. The van completed a full 180 degree spin
and launched backward into ravine. It crashed on its rear
thirty feet below in an explosion of crunching glass and

twisting metal that left its grill and single headlight pointed skyward.

H.I. didn't remember a whole section of fence collapsing and rotating out over the ravine. He didn't remember being in the way and didn't remember falling. He just knew that all of those things happened because he found himself hanging in space and holding on to two things at once, a piece of the fence and April.

"Oh, God! Oh, God!" April squeezed her arms around his waist, her legs kicking in space. He made sure she had a firm grip on him, then stuck his arm through a space between two broken boards and crooked his elbow like a hook. The pain lanced through his shoulder like a torch, and he knew he could not last long. He swung his free arm toward April.

"I want you to climb up my back and reach for a hand-hold in the fence."

"I hate heights, Tech."

"Then don't look down."

It was bad advice. Had she looked down, she would have seen the big man climb out of the cab and stand on the front grill. She would have pulled her legs out of his reach. But things didn't work out that way. The big man reached up and grabbed her ankle.

With the one headlight directly under him, the big man was just a shadow, but H.I. could see he was badly injured and in pain. On his own last shot of adrenalin, H.I. might have asked a last time what the big man was doing and why. But H.I. was too busy seeing that the big man was holding April with one hand and raising the Mac-10 upward with the other.

The gunfire filled H.I.'s ears.

Chapter Twelve

You never want to see anyone shot, H.I. would later tell himself. You never want to see anyone die. Because it's not like in the movies. It's not like the movies at all. It's not some special effect and not some stunt guy who'll get up later. There are no exploding chunks of flesh or spurting blood. The blood seeps out later, and there's not a whole lot because most of the bleeding is on the inside as a steel projectile splatters into fragments that tear up real human parts. And by then the dead person looks as cold as clay. That's the bad part.

The gunshots struck the big man in the head, thumped it only slightly, and crumpled him like a used rag doll. His head stopped rolling at the edge of the grill, his dead eyes open and his dark blood pooling on the single headlight.

"Dammit! H.I., I told you to wait at home."

Doc was suddenly on the ledge and lowering an arm. He hadn't done the shooting, and it took H.I. a second to get over the shock of seeing him. But Doc was no illusion. He was real and standing on the ledge next to a redheaded woman. She was the one who held an automatic pistol in her hand. She seemed pleased with herself, and H.I. knew there was something bad about her right away. She enjoyed killing the big man.

"You never listen." Doc grabbed H.I.'s free arm and helped him get his other arm loose from the fence boards. April still hung with her arms locked around H.I.'s waist and her head buried in the small of his back. She was shaking like crazy. H.I. threw his weight on Doc, got a foothold in the fence, and let April climb. Doc pulled her onto the ledge. Immediately, she did what H.I. wanted to do. She dropped to her knees and vomited. She was too shaken to ask him the obvious.

Doc wouldn't have answered anyway, H.I. told himself. Beside him, the redheaded woman slipped her pistol into a holster and closed her parka. She started to move, but stopped at the wail of the approaching sirens. She spoke to Doc. "Bethesda police."

"Thank God." April wiped her mouth and lifted her head. The redhead grabbed at April's wrist, pulled her upright.

"Wait just a damn minute!" April jerked back. "I want to know what's going on."

For a second H.I. missed the obvious, that the big man was somehow linked to both April and to Doc. That struck H.I. as impossible. April repeated her question, and waited for an answer. But the redhead wasn't going to give one.

"Some other damn minute, kid." The redhead motioned to Doc.

Doc led the way to a black van parked at the street and pointed April inside. She went protesting. H.I. followed. The redhead climbed in the driver's seat, started the van, and started moving before the last door slammed shut. She hit the gas, as a third approaching siren joined the others. She made a one-eighty-turn in the street and accelerated toward April's house.

Over Doc's shoulder and through the windshield, H.I. saw McCready's wrecked Plymouth. The windshield was gone, and the front end was spewing radiator steam up a tree. H.I. told Doc to stop. Doc shook his head and whispered that McCready was dead. So was the other man. H.I. felt bad about McCready and would have said something. But the sirens were getting closer, and redhead took that as a cue to step harder on the gas.

She stopped once at H.I.'s parked jeep. Doc popped his door release and gave H.I. an order. "Keys!"

H.I. gave them to him. Doc was in and out of the jeep in a few seconds, just long enough to retrieve his own duffel and H.I.'s. The redhead pulled away before Doc closed the door. She spun again and gunned toward the loop, as the approaching sirens got louder. At the loop, she clicked on her turn signal, slowed, and took her time.

She made her turn as the first police car shot by on the left. The police strobe flashed through the van windows and receded behind it. The siren faded. The redhead accelerated. She looked in her rearview mirror and seemed to notice that both H.I. and April were wet and trembling. She spoke in a soft voice, sounding maternal instead of homicidal. It was a kind and patient voice.

"There's a blanket and a thermos of coffee back there."

"I don't want it," April spoke up. "I want to know what the hell is going on and who you are."

"I'm Alex Malone. You can call me Malone."

"Let's get something straight, Malone…"

"Let's not, kid."

H.I. opened the thermos and drank. The coffee was black and strong. Mostly it was hot. He felt April trembling and covered her with the blanket. Blinking red lights from two more approaching squad cars lit up her face. She was wide-eyed, still in shock. The two squad cars sped by. The sirens were shrill.

"We'll have to take her with us. There's no time for a safe house," Doc said.

"Agreed." Malone drove the speed limit.

"I want to know what the hell is going on." April sat up straight.

Malone eyed her coldly in the rearview mirror. "Don't worry. I have clothes for you."

"Keep them. I want out of here."

"Impossible," Doc said softly. "There's a lot you don't know."

No shit, Doc! H.I. wanted to say, but didn't. He knew Doc wasn't going to say jack until the time of his choosing. April should have known too. But from what H.I. could tell, she wasn't thinking clearly. A last strobe shot by, probably from the dash on an unmarked car. Its siren faded. Malone listened and smiled in the rearview mirror.

April must have seen the look on Malone's face. "Why are we running from the police?"

Malone answered, "You'll hear it all, when the time is…"

"The time is now, Malone! Or I'm out of the back of this van at the first stop light."

"This involves your mother," Doc said. He caught April by surprise. She wrapped the blanket tighter under her chin. Underneath she began shaking again. H.I. could feel it. He slipped his arm around her and felt her sob.

H.I. told himself he should have figured it out a long time ago. The colder reality was that he actually had figured it out, but had never wanted to believe it. Dr. Kay did the same kind of work Doc did, contract work for secret employers within the government. That pissed H.I. off.

He hugged April and whispered, "Don't ask anything right now. Trust me. You don't want to know."

"I'd call that good advice, kid." Malone said it into the rearview mirror.

"Comes from experience," H.I answered. But actually what he'd done on previous jobs had been nothing like this. He just pretended that it had been. Maybe he was pretending to calm April. "I've done this before, unfortunately."

"I know you have," Malone's eyes returned to the road.

"This is bullshit!" April pulled away from H.I.

"No." He took another drink of coffee and looked at her. "You haven't seen bullshit yet."

Chapter Thirteen

The digging continued long after dark. It mixed with the distant, soft undulation of Wagner pouring from speakers along the perimeter fence. With every stab of steel into dirt, Dr. Kay winced, remembering Jennings and the others. She was relieved that she didn't have to watch them being dumped into the mass grave. She was mad at herself for feeling relieved. She tightened her hands around the steel bars of her cot.

For what seemed like the hundredth time, Bulldog offered her a cigar. She refused. He shrugged indifferently, bit off the end and spit it across the tent floor. He lit up and took a puff. The pungent smell filled the tent and stung her nostrils.

"You're missing a bloody fine cigar." He looked at her a long time. Too long.

She avoided his stare. She wrapped her knees in her arms and considered what she knew. More than two hundred mercenaries had arrived. They had a well-organized structure of command. Though she'd heard mostly Russian spoken, all of the mercenaries responded to English-speaking officers. They were extremely well-armed, and their weapons were standard issue for American marines: M16 assault rifles, Beretta M9 pistols, combat shotguns, MP5-N submachine guns, and M249 SAW machine guns. Their helicopters were old American Hueys and Cobra gunships.

Dr. Kay came up with two explanations. The first was the one she hoped to be true. The material and weapons were black market. The second made her very afraid. What if she was seeing a covert operation that had originated in the same building where'd she gotten her own orders?

A sick feeling came into her stomach. The covert operation made sense. It wouldn't be the first. Not by a long shot! Covert operations provided a lot of plausible deniability. If things went bad with Alpha Bell Tower, the Brazilians would have to look hard for someone to blame. A covert operation would also explain how Alpha Bell Tower's security had been breached. But it did not explain Victor Rykoff.

Rykoff was a wild card. His computer files made that clear. No matter how much money might be offered him, Rykoff would never work for the CIA or run a covert operation for the Pentagon. The files made it clear that Rykoff's agenda was much more complex and much more dangerous than money.

A distant explosion broke her chain of thought.

This one was much further away than the others had been. Shouts followed again, lasting until the tractor engines drowned them out. Dr. Kay sensed a pattern. First she'd hear the explosives, and then she'd hear the shouts and tractors. She reasoned what was being done. The forest was being cleared to the east, along the path of destruction scorched into the earth by Bell Tower in its final few seconds of flight. But why?

She waited for the digging to resume. But it stayed quiet, and she realized the digging was over. She felt another chill in her stomach. Thinking she would vomit, she buried her face in her hands. A voice made her look up.

"You are not doing your work, Frau Doktor Waterstone." Dr. Steiner was suddenly inside the tent and hovering over her. The tent's single gas lamp lit up the underside of his face and made shadows around his spectacles. He looked like a Halloween ghoul. "Rykoff made your position clear, Ja?"

"I made my position just as clear."

"You will come with me." Steiner nodded to Bulldog, who pulled Kay to her feet and shoved her out of the tent.

Outside, the floodlights hurt her eyes. She saw a half-dozen Jivanos under guard and smoothing dirt atop a mass grave. A mercenary in camouflage fatigues tried to pass them water in a bucket. The Jivanos ignored it. One Jivano raised a squat face toward Dr. Kay. Framed in black paint, the Jivano's eyes were frighteningly calm.

"The savage thinks the end is near, Ja?" Steiner cackled.

Dr. Kay looked away and followed Bulldog. Garbled radio voices from handheld radios came from every direction. The mercenaries had rebuilt the cyclone fence and run wires from the auxiliary generator to electrify it. Large bunkers had been dug and fortified with sandbags, each protecting a section of fence. They were secure enough to withstand an air assault, Dr. Kay reasoned. Nearby, she recognized crates loaded with Stinger missiles, and beyond the crates, she saw the jeep-like profile of an Avenger anti-aircraft vehicle and its launch tubes. She knew that low-flying, friendly aircraft wouldn't expect the Stingers and wouldn't survive them.

"Keep moving, my little China." Bulldog forced her along faster. She stumbled behind him, studying the terrain.

Beyond the fence perimeter, to the north and south, small teams of mercenaries were laying mines. To the east of the compound, floods lighted flat terrain mostly cleared of the trees Alpha Bell Tower had burned and flattened on its approach. Where there had been stumps and massive fallen trunks, Bulldozers and Jivanos were cleaning the earth. Overlooking them, a bare metal tower was erected. It supported a radar dish.

She glanced west only once. The complex was intact, its entry airlock closed. A lone sentry leaned against the railing of the entry stairs and smoked a cigarette. His weapon was slung. He looked bored.

Bulldog led Dr. Kay south. Steiner followed on her heels. They passed the control complex, then a fortified bunker where the communications dish had been moved. She counted several additional dishes, noting that they were all aimed in the direction of different communications satellites. The bunker was roofed by composite covered in camouflage netting. Beyond the communications bunker, a larger bunker was dug into the earth and walled in sandbags. Steiner stepped up his pace and descended into the bunker ahead of Bulldog. Dr. Kay followed at his back, stepping down into an interior lit by red bulbs meant to preserve night vision.

"Take a seat, Dr. Waterstone." Rykoff was waiting in front of a dim television. He patted the steel chair next to his, indicating she should sit. "Dr. Steiner tells me you are not being cooperative."

"I told you I wouldn't cooperate" She remained standing. Bulldog nudged her forward. In spite of herself, she glanced sideways and saw the blue glow of the television reflect from Rykoff's face. Its hideousness still shocked her.

She turned away but couldn't escape the sound of his breathing. It was heavy and course. Maybe the damage to his face extended to the soft tissues of his throat. Maybe when he'd masqueraded as Smith, his facial prosthetics supported his trachea. Maybe without the prosthetics, he was vulnerable. She promised herself she'd make use of that vulnerability.

"Have a seat." Rykoff's voice was gentle.

Dr. Kay did as she was told and faced the television. On screen, CNN was being fed from a satellite. The volume was muted. Rykoff turned it up and spoke. "You'll find this next piece interesting."

On screen, the correspondent wore an overcoat and stood outside in the cold. Behind him, Dr. Kay could see yellow police tape, lights, and uniforms. She was looking at a street and pine woods. The wreckage of an old white station wagon was barely visible, smashed against a big tree. She didn't recognize the car. But there was something familiar about the street. And suddenly she knew it was more than familiar. Nausea gripped her from belly to throat, but she had nothing to vomit . The correspondent looked confused. "The quiet in this small suburban neighborhood of Washington DC was shattered tonight by a shoot-out and car chase that has left four people dead, two of them confirmed to be federal agents."

At the correspondent's back, police parted to make way for a plainclothes detective leading a woman by the arm. Dr. Kay saw the woman and felt her insides turn to ice. In the TV lights, Dottie Sinclair looked as if she' been crying. Dr. Kay watched helplessly.

"An affluent neighborhood," the correspondent said. "It's not supposed to happen here." He stepped directly in front of the camera. "Many questions are still unanswered, and still missing is a resident of this affluent neighborhood, sixteen-year-old April Waterstone."

A black-and-white photo from April's high school yearbook flashed on the screen. It hung there a second, while another voice announced that there would be a special on the spread of teen violence and automatic weapons.

Dr. Kay felt the blood drain out of her face. Her legs buckled. For a minute, she thought she would faint. She tightened her calves and recovered.

The anchor and the local correspondent shared a split screen.

"Which federal agency was involved? Was this some sort of investigation into illegal weapons?"

"Automatic weapons were used. At present, there's no federal agency coming forward with information, though sources inside the local police say that the two federal agents worked for the CIA. As you know, the CIA is prohibited by law from domestic activities. And interestingly, more than one congressman lives in this neighborhood..."

Rykoff turned off the set and spun slowly toward Dr. Kay. His violet eyes were calm, almost hypnotic. "Your daughter is lovely, Dr. Waterstone. I can't wait to meet her."

Dr. Kay knew what she wanted to do, what she had to do. But it was beyond her, beyond anyone. The words came out by themselves in a voice she recognized but could no longer control. "I'll do anything you want," she heard herself say. "Just promise me you won't hurt her."

Chapter Fourteen

H.I. knew where Malone and Doc were taking them. At least he knew their first stop. It was a given. April figured it out and tensed under the blanket as soon as she saw the strobes from low-flying planes. She leaned close to H.I. and whispered. She was afraid.

"They said they were going to take me to the airport."

"Who?"

"Jack and Spud! Those creeps at the house. They said they were taking me to the airport. Here I am at the airport. This feels wrong."

"No. This is okay." H.I. lied. It wasn't okay at all.

"How do you know?"

Malone made a sudden turn. Her headlights swept an empty two-lane road and a high cyclone fence. Beyond the fence, blue runway lights stretched into darkness. H.I. could tell it was a small, private airfield. The approaching jets screamed overhead just above the treetops. They shook the van.

"This feels wrong." April whispered, nodding toward Malone. "I don't trust that bitch."

"You trust me?"

She turned her head toward H.I. in the dark and looked in his direction a long time without talking. He guessed that she was remembering that something about him that he wanted her to forget. He wanted to forget it himself. After a damn long pause, she returned to the matter at hand. "You said you've done this before."

"Yeah." He lied again.

For sure, Doc had taken him on some pretty crummy jobs in some pretty awful places with some pretty scary people. And probably some of those scary people would love hearing that the two of them were dead. But dodging bullets? No way! And Doc had always been the one running the show, no matter how many government types were involved. Anyone who didn't agree with him was someone he dismissed without hesitation. But this time Doc was reacting, not leading. He was letting Malone make all of the first moves, a clear violation of his big rule: be in charge! It was the heart of what Doc called controlled risk. H.I.'d always argued that the control part was impossible. Risk might be calculated but never controlled. But just try telling Doc that perfect control was impossible. He'd fire you. Yet here Doc was, letting Malone take the lead and make the calls. And from what H.I. had seen of Malone, that seemed like a bad idea.

H.I. could have told April as much, but sitting next to her in the back of that van, he lied. He figured she needed the confidence. She'd especially need it if the two of them, he and April, were going to make a break. And H.I. was thinking long and hard about making a break.

"Yeah, I've done this before." H.I. said.

She didn't answer him and didn't relax, either. She kept her eyes on Malone as Malone pulled into a small driveway near a hanger. Malone stopped the van at a security box fitted to a high cyclone gate and pressed the call button. The voice that answered was a woman. The woman sounded bored.

"Number, please."

"644 Papa X-ray," Malone gave the tail number of an aircraft.

"Have a nice night."

An electronic hum preceded the clanking motor that opened the gate sideways. It closed as soon as Malone drove the van inside. Malone accelerated directly toward a twin engine corporate jet lighted up by the lamps in the cockpit and cabin. The tail number was N644PX. Malone stopped the van behind the left wing and opened April's door. The interior lights lit Malone's small face as she turned to April and raised an eyebrow. "You'll find a green duffel in the back of the cabin. Help yourself to warm clothes."

"I want to know where we're going." April hugged herself in her blanket.

"I know you do," was all Malone answered. She waited while April and H.I. climbed out of the van.

I'll tell you when we're in the air," Doc shot April a look. "I promise."

Malone and Doc left H.I. and April on the tarmac and drove in the direction of the hanger beside the main gate. H.I. waited until the van was parked at the hanger. He judged the distance to the airfield's entrance and figured that running in the dark, April and he could make their exit in under a minute. After that, he'd know lots of places to lay low until whatever job Doc was doing with Malone reached its conclusion.

The thought of laying low with April was overpowering. He'd be saving her life and his own. The two of them would have time to talk, maybe clear the air about things. No doubt about it. Just being on the run together would be its own reward. And it was a logical thing to do.

But April might not want to run for it at all.

Knowing that her mother was in danger, April was unlikely to simply run away. On that score, H.I. couldn't blame her. But he also knew Dr. Kay would want her to run like hell. There was no freaking way Dr. Kay would want April along on this job or keeping company with Malone. Dr. Kay's first choice for April would be a safe house. But now that a safe house was impossible, she'd want April on the run with H.I. Of course, convincing April of that would be damn difficult.

For one thing, April would call him a coward for even suggesting they run. Big fricking deal! Wouldn't be the worst name H.I. had ever been called. The coward charge wasn't true, and it wouldn't stick. Not once April thought about things. And while she was thinking about things, it would have to occur to her that her being with Malone might actually increase the danger in her mother's situation. As a bonus, April would realize that her jumping ship would totally piss off Malone. That alone ought to make April fricking ecstatic.

But there'd still be a question that H.I. would have to ask himself. Was he running out on Doc? He had to believe he wasn't. On this job, he'd only be bringing limited skills to the table when it came to dealing with threat to life and limb. Sure, on previous jobs there had been weapons pointed and threats made. But no bloodshed. Contrast that with this job. Not even on the road yet and this one was loaded with bloodshed. Not the usual Tech father and son scientific outing. And in truth, something worse was at play.

The truth was that Doc wasn't thinking clearly. So far all of Doc's moves had been bad ones. He'd run from a shooting, avoided the police, and was now cramming all of the witnesses into a flight piloted by the shooter. And if that flight were to just happen to vanish, everything would be very neatly cleaned up. Doc was not processing on this one at all. So now it was H.I.'s job to do it for him. H.I. promised himself his moves would be good ones, not bad ones.

The first good move would be to take April and run. Hide her and make her safe. The second good move would be to cover Doc's back. Use McCready's work number to contact the CIA in a series of short calls from public phones. Choose phones in crowded places where there were multiple exits. Department stores were good. So were train stations, bus stations, restaurants, and street phones. Make it clear to the CIA that if anything happened to Doc or Dr. Kay, H.I. would be calling the DC police and the press. Let the CIA know that they should put a serious restraint on Malone's trigger finger. Let the CIA know that their win-win would be keeping Doc and Dr. Kay off any of Malone's future body counts.

H.I. took a second look at the jet and assured himself that neither he nor April would be riding it. But a shadow moving inside the cockpit told him otherwise.

The shadow was big and looking back at him. One guy, H.I. figured. Had to be an associate of Malone and had to be expecting April and him. Not the time to make a move with April.

H.I. picked up his duffel and Doc's. He led April under the wing and up the ladder through the jet's forward door. The two of them entered through a galley aft of the cockpit. April did not recognize the man in the cockpit. H.I. did.

Mid-thirties, H.I guessed. Powerful build but restrained manners. Pleasant enough facial features but still plain enough not to be noticed in a crowd or remembered two seconds after being seen. H.I. might have forgotten him too, had it not been for the when and where they had formerly crossed paths. When had been last summer just before the arrival of RM 1999. Where had been behind the wheel of the government sedan taking Dr. Kay from her driveway.

The man diverted his gaze to his instruments, but H.I. sensed he was aware of H.I.'s and April's every move from his peripheral vision. CIA ghost was written all over him. Outrunning this guy with April in tow was going to be tough. H.I. began to modify his plan.

"Good to see you again," H.I. said.

The man nodded and bent over instrumentation that was mostly displayed on small computer screens arranged in T- configuration The warning lights, switches, and throttles were uncluttered. The man worked the instruments with one eye while keeping the other eye on the two of them.

"Is this what they mean by glass cockpit?" H.I. asked.

"That's right". The man acted as if he didn't remember their first encounter. But H.I. was damn sure the man did remember.

"This must be a new G4."

"No. It's a G5."

"My name's H.I." H.I. stuck out his hand. "I didn't get your name."

"Ramsey." The man shook H.I.'s hand without turning around. His grip was dry and quick, released and back to his instruments in a second.

"We've met before, you know?"

"Not likely. I'd remember." The man toggled the hydraulics and fuel indicators on one of the computer screens. "You should get settled."

H.I. led April aft into the cabin. She picked up Malone's duffel, disappeared into the lavatory, and clicked the door lock. H.I. peeled off his wet clothes and found dry ones inside his duffel: Adams Day sweatshirt, khakis, and running shoes. He felt warm for the first time in over and hour. He took the nearest chair, a soft leather swivel that could be reclined for sleeping. The only aircraft exit was at Ramsey's back, just aft of the cockpit. H.I. spun in the chair and looked out of the window.

Doc and Malone were still nowhere in sight. The field entrance was maybe a hundred yards away. Next to the cyclone fence, there'd be an inside switch box that opened the gate. The gate would slide open wide enough for a person in a few seconds. H.I. thought about Dr. Kay, reminding himself that she'd want him to get April in the clear.

He spun toward the aft lavatory and saw that April was taking her time inside. There was no question about what to do. Knock on the door and coax her out. Tell Ramsey the two of them were stepping out to stretch before the flight. Step outside and run. It was the right thing to do. No question about it. Doc and Dr. Kay would be okay, no matter what he did.

H.I. took a long look at the hundred yards between the plane and the gate and studied a path that would use parked planes for cover. They'd lose Ramsey in the dark.

They'd bum a ride on the outside road. There would be places in the city to hide for a while. All the two of them had to do was make that first move. It was now or never. He thought again about Dr. Kay, maybe in trouble in some crummy place. He knew what he was going to do.

He reclined his chair and waited for Doc and Malone to return.

A jeep driven by a man in mechanic's fatigues approached the left-wing tip and idled. Doc and Malone got out. Malone carried a small, hard suitcase. Doc carried his laptop. The mechanic drove the jeep away. The navigation lights on the wings blinked on as soon as Malone and Doc climbed up the ladder. Malone shut the door and climbed into the left cockpit seat. She donned a radio headset. She and Ramsey ran a checklist.

Doc bent over the swivel chair and handed H.I. a passport. Inside the cover, April's high school yearbook photo was fixed to the paper. Doc seemed pleased. "Not bad for an hour's work."

One of Malone's fellow CIA ghosts had entered the crime scene at April's home and copied her yearbook photo with a digital camera. He'd sent the data over his cell phone to Langley, where a computer had reconfigured the photo to the proper size and relayed it to Malone at the air field. She'd stuck it into a blank passport book and filled in the data with a special printer.

"Probably won't need it anyway." Doc placed the passport in his jacket. His remark said a lot of bad things about where they'd be going. Had to be like all the others they'd visited.

"Shit!" H.I. clenched his teeth. "Some third-world toilet."

"Watch your language, H.I."

The turbofan jet engines fired up loud, first the right and then the left. Doc took a seat and opened his laptop. April clicked open the lavatory door and exited. She was dressed in jeans and a sweater meant for a smaller woman. H.I. guessed they belonged to Malone. April dropped into a swivel chair and began brushing thick blond hair over her shoulders. She was beautiful to watch, brushing her hair like that.

"Don't stare. It's rude." Her eyes were beautiful blue storms. They narrowed.

H.I. looked away.

"I didn't say you couldn't look at me."

H.I. told himself he could look at her the rest of his life. On Doc's order, she buckled her seat belt. She asked him about Dr. Kay.

"Later." Doc didn't look up from his laptop.

The cabin lights dimmed, and the tail strobe reflected from water puddles in the tarmac. The turbofans were throttled up. The G5 taxied fast and shot steeply from the runway, climbing like a rocket. Over the back of his shoulder, H.I. saw the lights of Dulles and DC plummet into darkness and vanish in less than a minute. The G5 climbed above silver clouds and nosed into level flight somewhere between forty and fifty thousand feet.

Outside the right window, H.I. found Polaris, the North Star, hovering above the western horizon. Ursa Minor, the little dipper, was lower than Ursa Major, the big dipper. The G5 was heading southeast. H.I. checked his heading against the GPS-fed global positioning display on the monitor fixed to the forward bulkhead. Heading southeast was correct. Kudos to Marsden for making him learn some astronomy.

"Time to talk." April loosened her belt and stared at Doc. "Where are we going?"

"The Brazilian rain forest." Doc rebooted his laptop. "More specifically, the upper Amazon basin."

As if on cue, the monitors on the forward and aft bulkheads changed. The numbers indicating heading, altitude, and ground speed vanished. Maps appeared, and flight paths superimposed over them as red lines. The flight paths dipped southeast over the Atlantic, skirted the eastern tip of Puerto Rico, and angled south across Venezuela into Brazil. Icons appeared representing the plane's position. New number displays appeared beneath the maps. The distance along the flight path was 3952 miles. Air speed was five hundred knots. H.I. did his own math, hoping it was wrong. He knew it wasn't.

"Another damn all-night flight." He pulled his books out of his duffel.

"What do you think you're doing? April asked.

"Finals are next week. Remember those?" Actually he wasn't interested in his finals. Clayfield had already made it clear that he was going to be expelled from Adams Day. But no big deal. He had time now to straighten out things with April. And his school path would take care of itself no matter where he attended. That much was clear. H.I.'s real concern was the decision he'd made not to grab April and run. He was having buyers regret, having it big time. So he needed distraction and hence his books.

"Study now?" April shot him a disbelieving look.

"I won't get the chance later." H.I. looked across the aisle. "Will I, Doc?"

"No." Doc stood and moved toward the cockpit. April waited until he was out of earshot, then turned to H.I.

"You're not an ordinary nerd, Tech. You're a fugitive from the *Twilight Zone*." She stared in the direction Doc had gone. "And so is he."

"No argument there."

She turned in her seat and stared out of the left side of the plane. For a minute, H.I. could have sworn she was crying and trying to hide it. Thousands of feet below, the clouds broke into wisps. In the star light, the sea was silver and calm.

"Want something to eat?" H.I. asked.

"No way, Tech." Maybe she was going to say something worse, but she caught herself and smiled apologetically. "No, thanks."

H.I. moved to the kitchenette behind the cockpit and rummaged through the small refrigerator. The sandwiches were the prepackaged kind that came out of a machine. Next to them were chips and a half-dozen cans of soda. He pretended to rummage and kept an ear pointed toward the cockpit where Ramsey was doing the talking.

"First Caracas." Ramsey raised his voice above the turbo-fan jets. "We check things out there first. Then we move on to Manaus and pick up a boat. We can be on-site in three or four days."

"We don't have the time, and Manaus is a very bad idea." Doc sounded impossibly sure of himself.

"What's wrong with Manaus?" Malone asked.

"Time, for one thing." Doc answered like he was ready to take charge. "Your satellite photos for another. They show two sea-going freighters anchored at Manaus."

"Their registration checks out fine," Ramsey cut in.

"Irrelevant. They arrived together two days before *you lost* Bell Tower." He paused and continued. "We have to assume a security problem at Bell Tower. By extension, everything in Manaus is suspect."

"What's your alternative, Dr. Tech?" Malone's temper was rising.

"We put down in Villa Lobos," Doc said.

"Shit!" Ramsey raised his voice.

"Not unless you're in hurry to kill yourself." Malone added.

"Are you afraid of Villa Lobos, Malone?" Doc asked.

"I know what this airplane can and can't do." Malone wasn't backing down. "I know Villa Lobos is a short strip built for a lot less airplane. You think of that, Doctor?"

"I think of everything, including our estimated fuel consumption, our estimated weight on arrival, wind velocities and direction this time of the year, plus the performance capability of the G5 and the skill of the pilot."

"Ever think you could be wrong?"

"Only about the skill of the pilot." Doc exited the cockpit and winked as he slipped around H.I., who pretended to be making a choice, ham and cheese or turkey. H.I. opened a coke, took a sip, and listened to the cockpit.

"Someone at the company's got a seriously sick sense of humor," Malone said.

"I'm that someone, Malone," Ramsey answered.

"You used to have better judgment."

"He's the right outside consultant for this problem. Believe that."

"Shit, Ramsey. Shit!"

"Cool it, Malone. Tell me what happened back there on the ground."

"Someone tried to grab the girl. Two friendlies are dead."

"McCready and Hitchcock! Damn!" Ramsey said. There was silence for a few seconds, the bad kind of seconds when someone knows he's screwed up but doesn't know how. Somehow it was reassuring to H.I. to see that Ramsey had the capacity for guilt. Ramsey spoke again. "Damn! I asked Hitchcock to go along, but I didn't think…"

"We've got a leak somewhere." Malone said what H.I. suspected Ramsey was probably thinking.

H.I. chose a ham sandwich. It was hard to mess up a ham sandwich. He moved aft and found Doc and April talking. Actually, Doc was doing the talking, and April was doing the sobbing. Doc was probably telling her what little he wanted her to know about the kind of work he and apparently Dr. Kay did. April was probably finding those things tough to believe. H.I. sort of knew the feeling.

H.I. took a forward seat, clicked on his reading lamp, and dug into Shakespeare. He really was supposed to prep for finals. He was supposed to study *Richard III*, but murder and ambition were not on his wish list that night. He found himself off track and deep in *The Tempest*, a play not even in the school curriculum. Focus was always a big problem for H.I. But there was *The Tempest*, and it had everything someone like him could want: a shipwreck,

a beautiful damsel in distress, love at first sight, a magician, and a monster.

Doc ripped the book out of his hands. "Shakespeare
hasn't published recently," he said. "The Department of
Defense has."

Doc handed him a laptop with discs marked only by a
red serial number. H.I. ignored them. Doc spoke up, sounding pissed. "Aren't you even curious?"

"Sure, Doc! Loads!" H.I. booted up the laptop, inserted
the disc, and entered the password Doc gave him. The
unexpected happened. The first file got his attention.

EYES ONLY
FROM J. RAMSEY
TO CHAIRMAN SENATE INTELLIGENCE COMMITTEE
DATE JULY 1999
SUBJECT: SUMMARY STATUS PROGECT ALPHA BELL TOWER

The file contained over a dozen memos and communications, all dated July 1999, all making references to Raymond Marsden. H.I. got a sick feeling in his gut, sick and
angry at the same time. Marsden had been ridiculed in
front of the entire planet. He'd ended up jumping from
his hotel room. And here Marsden was the subject of a top-
secret file. Maybe Marsden knew. Maybe it was in his mind
as he hurtled twelve floors to the pavement outside of the
DC Marriott.

H.I. read on. The file referred to his discovery, RM 1999,
but gave it a new designation assigned immediately after
the thing came down in the Amazon. Someone somewhere
at NASA dubbed it IMPACTOR ALPHA BELL TOWER.
Designation "impactor" referred to any comet, meteorite,
or asteroid that impacted the Earth.

H.I. moved to File 2, a study commissioned by NASA and later filed by the NSA and CIA.

TO: NASA
FROM: SG RESEARCH
SUBJECT: ASTEROID AND COMET COLLISION WITH EARTH
ASTEROIDS AND COMETS SMALLER THAN THREE HUNDRED FEET IN DIAMETER DO LITTLE DAMAGE. OUR BEST PREDICTION IS THAT SUCH OBJECTS SHOULD IMPACT WITH ENERGY EQUIVALENT TO THE HIROSHIMA BOMB.

H.I. guessed that Hiroshima could be minimal if it was not your personal address. Maybe destruction was like real estate, a matter of location, location, location. The report's author estimated the arrival of over five hundred such impactors in the next thousand years. He wrote *MOST WILL SIMPLY BREAK UP IN THE UPPER ATMOSPHERE. THOSE THAT REACH THE GROUND WILL EITHER VAPOR-IZE OR MIX WITH TARGET ROCKS.* The author's conclusion recommended against increased efforts to detect such objects on their approach. Not worth the effort, the author said.

Lucky Marsden! His find was the result of no increased efforts. But Marsden wasn't the only one who got lucky. H.I. found that out in File 3.

Other authorities picked up RM 1999 on its approach. Maybe they were inside the loop. Maybe they were the same experts who went live on Larry King to tell the world Marsden was wrong. Who knows? Either way, their work referenced a report from the Jet Propulsion Laboratory in California. Its data came from two places, the Arecibo Observatory in Puerto Rico and the Goldstone Solar System Radar in California.

SUBJECT: ASTEROID RADAR RESEARCH
METHOD: 1. ECHO POWER SPECTRA
        2.DELAY-DOPPLER VELOCITY MEASUREMENTS
TARGET: RM 1999

H.I. stared a long time, looking at images of RM 1999 in space and on approach. It wasn't an image of RM 1999 in the flesh. The image was a radar-derived shape model, something a computer created using radar echoes reflected from the object. The model was nothing to look at, just shadows along two axes on graph paper. But the model was doing something that space objects were not supposed to do. It was changing shape.

H.I. skipped the technical stuff and moved to File 4. The data came from a NASA satellite, the orbiting Compton Gamma Ray Observatory, whose position was changed to study RM 1999 on final approach. Onboard the satellite was the Oriented Scintillation Spectrometer Experiment, a machine that could measure gamma emissions. It measured RM 1999's emission particles at 511,000 electron volts. A smoking gun, the report concluded. A smoking gun for what happens when electrons meet positrons. Positrons do have another name that everyone knows: antimatter!

RM 1999, aka Alpha Bell Tower, was loaded with antimatter.

And Alpha Bell Tower did not break apart in the upper atmosphere. Nor did it vaporize on impact or melt into the target rocks. Nor did it impact with the energy of the Hiroshima bomb or leave a circular crater. Impactor Alpha Bell Tower touched ground in the upper Amazon basin, just south of the Guyana highlands and inside Brazil. It dug a wedge-shaped crater consistent with level flight. It remained completely intact.

Designation changed a second time. *Impactor* Alpha Bell Tower became *Object* Alpha Bell Tower.

A status summary followed. It made mention of ETRAC but did not elaborate the meaning of those initials. What was ETRAC? H.I. suspected some kind of think tank. Its members wrote the conclusions and recommendations.

DISPOSITION: FOR REASONS OF NATIONAL SECURITY, THE AREA SURROUNDING OBJECT ALPHA BELL TOWER HAS BEEN QUARANTINED AND REMANDED TO FURTHER INVESTIGATION PER ETRAC. THE BRAZILIAN GOVERNMENT IS IN FULL COOPERATION. SAID SECURITY ARRANGEMENTS AND QUARANTINE ARE BEING ARRANGED JOINTLY.

H.I. moved to the next file, but only got as far as the heading. He read it twice to make sure he was not seeing things. Then he looked across the aisle at April. Her face was turned toward the window. Her reading lamp was out. He turned again and read the heading. It sent chills into his stomach. The plurality of the second word implied that what followed was something known, not a hypothetical *if.*

SUBJECT: EXTRATERRESTIAL LIFEFORMS

Chapter Fifteen

"They do have self-contained air, don't they?" Dr. Kay tried to keep her eyes locked on the central monitor. But she couldn't help glancing toward Rykoff.

"Of course they do," Rykoff answered. "We learned by your mistake." Wearing a communication headset, he spun in his chair. His eyes were deep violet, almost soothing. The rest of his face was a twisted, hideous reminder of the monster inside.

Dr. Kay darted her eyes to avoid looking at him.

She looked beyond banks of computers, monitors, and technicians in headsets. Rykoff's technicians had modified the entire service module. She found the screen she wanted. It was fed by a camera inside Node 2, where a half-dozen men led by Dr. Steiner were climbing into level A protective gear.

She felt Rykoff's eyes watching her. She narrowed her vision and shut him out.

On screen, she saw the vapro-proof lime-green suits take the form of their human occupants. The suits were rear-entry and fully encapsulated with attached sock boots and glove units. The hoods were four times the size of a human head, fronted by twin-layer face shields made of PVC and Teflon. The large hoods gave their occupants a simian appearance. Underneath the hood, each man wore a self-contained breathing apparatus fed by compressed air carried on his back. All were armed. Their equipment was packaged in steel suitcases.

"Tell them to be damn careful." Dr. Kay unconsciously stepped closer to her own monitor. She pulled up the infra-red feed and locked on Alpha Bell Tower, a motionless yellow orb in sea of swirling gray. The yellow was Jenning's choice, she remembered. Yellow like his Volkswagen bug. Now Jennings was in the earth decomposing. She shoved the thought from her mind and watched the Bell Tower orb. It seemed to be waiting. She spoke loudly, feeling the fear in her voice. "There can't be so much as one minor scratch in their clothing. Not one breech."

"My dear Dr. Waterstone. You worry too much." Rykoff patted the empty steel chair beside him. "Take the co-command mic."

Dr. Kay dropped into the chair, brushed black hair from her face, and fitted a headset. Bulldog hovered at her back. Unlike Rykoff, he stank of cigars and body odor.

"You're nervous, Doctor." Rykoff spoke without looking at her.

"Any sane person would be."

"How many of your people did it kill?"

"The whole team."

Rykoff laughed. "You were lucky it killed them before they had time to bring it out of the crater."

Dr. Kay felt the tears and pressure damn up behind her eyes. It had not been luck. It had been a mistake, her mistake.

"Dugout, this is Batter. Do you copy?" An orange-hooded head filled the central monitor. Behind the hood's clear PVC and Teflon face shield, Steiner's face came into view. His nose and mouth were covered in tight-fitting, black breathing gear. His eyes were covered in thick spectacles and looked like they were swimming in fishbowls.

"Copy, Batter." Rykoff answered. "Check your com links."

"Copy, Dugout. My count."

Each of Steiner's team members spoke his call sign into his mic. Each used a baseball position, starting with catcher and working around the infield.

"You are go, Pitcher."

Dr. Kay watched an overhead monitor change feeds. On screen Steiner and his team moved through a naked steel module fitted with shower nozzles. At the module's far end, they vanished single file through a heavy hatch. Steiner was last, cranking the hatch shut behind him. The monitor changed feeds to the next module. More naked steel. Over-cover suits of aluminized Kevlar were hanging on rods. Steiner's team removed the suits and struggled into them. Dr. Kay considered the multiple levels of protection. There was no guarantee that the protection would matter.

"This is insane!" Dr. Kay shook her head. She remembered her own team and felt her stomach fill with ice.

On screen, Steiner took the lead through another hatch. Dr. Kay's ears filled with clacking from a keyboard, and the camera feeds changed again. On the monitor, she found herself staring lengthwise down an accordion tunnel made of polymer interwoven with steel ribs. Inside the tunnel hanging light bulbs threw shadows. Between the bulbs the passage was too dark to see. Dr. Steiner's team began a descent, following the tunnel downward until it passed a Y intersection with a second tunnel.

Dr. Kay knew the second tunnel was the way back. It made a turn upward and interfaced with Node 3 on the far side of the isolation lab module. The second tunnel was to be used to bring specimens to the isolation lab itself. By either route, first or second tunnel, workers were to use the decontamination showers before reentering Node 2.

"Pitcher, this is dugout." Rykoff used his mic. "Put your A cam on point."

"Copy, Dugout." Steiner answered. "Cam to point."

Dr. Kay heard more keyboard clacking. The monitor changed feeds again and filled with a jerky image transmitted from a hand camera. The camera was being carried down the tunnel beyond the intersection. It was stopped at the tunnel mouth and pointed outward. She knew what lay beyond. She told herself she couldn't look.

"Your turn." Rykoff spoke to her. She turned toward his face. His eyes were penetrating, studying her from head to foot. She cringed and made herself look back at the screen.

The image fed from outside the tunnel mouth. It was darkness and frozen fog.

"Your turn, Dr. Waterstone." Rykoff's voice was almost gentle.

"This is Dugout." Dr. Kay managed to speak into her mic. "Move straight ahead about two hundred yards. Angle your lights down. Otherwise they'll reflect back in your eyes. Watch your step."

Lights arced ahead of the hand-held camera lens. The lights swept an uneven white surface dropping into dense fog. Drizzle was falling in all directions.

"Surface crunches underfoot, Dugout." Steiner radioed. "It's slick."

Another voice followed Steiner's. "Is cold as Siberian winter down here. Air reads minus ten degrees centigrade. No, floor is even colder. Floor reads minus seventy-eight."

Dr. Kay turned to Rykoff. "The whole floor of the crater is covered in dry ice."

He nodded back.

She swallowed. "At first, we thought a comet had come down, like the one that leveled the Tunguska River forest in 1908. We thought RM 1999 was just a comet that dug a crater and layered it with frozen remains. Comet gasses are hydrogen and methyl cyanide. We thought maybe Bell Tower was a large comet and that poison gas killed everything. But…"

"But you were wrong."

Dr. Kay nodded.

Rykoff pointed to the infrared monitor. Alpha Bell Tower's yellow orb was completely still. "Your so-called comet shattered on impact and left behind a solid core. An event never before observed!"

"Comets do not have solid cores." Dr. Kay answered. "It's not a comet."

"You were wrong about the poison gas too."

She nodded again. Spectroscopy had shown that the only unusual element in the dense cloud surrounding Alpha Bell Tower was an exceptionally high amount of carbon dioxide. The significance had not been lost on her.

Water vapor was a known interstellar molecule. It had been identified in space, along with carbon monoxide and another four dozen, mostly toxic chemicals. But never carbon dioxide, not in interplanetary space.

Oxygen was going into Bell Tower and carbon dioxide was coming out. The *process* implied life. It was the *process* that mattered. The planet Venus was loaded with carbon dioxide in an atmosphere ninety-five times as dense as Earth's, devoid of oxygen and hotter than the boiling point of water. Not a place to *process* life. Alpha Bell Tower was different. It was using oxygen and producing carbon dioxide.

Squeezed to pressures of a thousand pounds per square inch, carbon dioxide turns to liquid. Released and allowed to rapidly evaporate, it instantly loses its heat with the escaping gas and leaves behind its solid, frozen form. Something inside Alpha Bell Tower was creating those pressures on a massive scale and extruding the frozen solid. Contact with the warm air produced the dense fog and constant drizzle.

Something inside Alpha Bell Tower was alive. Something had killed all Earth life within a one-mile radius of the crash site. Something had killed the team Dr. Kay had allowed into the crater. Her fault, she reminded herself.

"This is Pitcher." Steiner's voice came over the radio headset and wall speakers. "Geiger reads 100 millirads."

"Affirmative, Pitcher." Rykoff answered. "That's normal background. It agrees with our readings."

"Give us a sweep with the GID-3." Dr. Kay spoke into her mic.

On screen, one of the men opened a suitcase and activated a box-sized piece of equipment. A second man swept the air with an attached sensor that looked like a stubby weapon. The data fed into Dr. Kay's computer screen.

```
IONIC MOBILE SPECTROSCOPY
MUSTARD AGENTS    conc. 000
SARIN             conc. 000
SOMAN             conc. 000
TABUN             conc. 000
```

Rykoff turned to Kay. "No poison gasses."

"No manmade nerve gasses or blistering agents. The key word is manmade." She punched her keyboard, sending new instructions to the mobile unit.

```
HYDROGEN...........
HELIUM ...............
OXYGEN..............
CARBON..............
NITROGEN............
SULFUR ...............
```

"As I said." Rykoff watched as the software analyzed the concentrations. "There is nothing but air and a high level of carbon dioxide. No poison gasses and no excess radiation. Two killers eliminated."

"This is Dugout." Dr. Kay ignored him and spoke slowly into her mic. "Check your suit pressures and sound off. Tell me if anything hurts."

The pressures came back in the green. No one reported pain, just intense cold. On Dr. Kay's direction, Steiner ordered First Base and Second Base to dig under the dry ice. It was deep.

The radio voice came back garbled. "There's something hard under the ice. It looks like a piece of tree, but it's hard as rock."

"Watch that edge. It's sharp." The second voice was garbled too.

Watching the screen, Rykoff ordered a technician to run a system check on the radio. The distortion in the radio voices became more pronounced. Just as suddenly, the voices cleared.

On screen, one of the suited figures was lifting something. "That's not wood. It looks like animal bone. Yes! Definitely bone fragments. They're heavy." He paused. "Like a piece of rock."

"Put it down! Do it now!" Dr. Kay shouted into her mic, then covered it and turned to Rykoff. "It's all fossilized, the plant life, the animal life, the whole forest. The soft tissues are gone. Some of the harder stuff absorbed minerals from the soil and fossilized. That kind of thing should never have happened. Frozen under the ice like that, the soft tissues, the whole animal or plant, should be preserved. But they're gone, stripped to the bone. The bone absorbed minerals from the soil, and all that's left are fossils."

Rykoff answered. "Defies nature, doesn't it?" He glued his eyes to the screen. "Nothing mineralizes that fast."

"That's right."

"It killed everything."

"Including my team."

Rykoff spoke into his microphone. "Place your markers. Continue your descent."

On the monitor Dr. Kay saw Steiner's team plant steel poles topped by battery-driven lights. Slowly they continued down into the darkness over the ice.

"Can you imagine the terror this will create once it becomes a weapon?" Rykoff whispered to Dr. Kay. He let one eye wander to the technician on his immediate right. The technician was mapping the path into the crater.

Dr. Kay looked at her keyboard. She knew what lay only yards ahead of Steiner's team. She did not want to look. But it was her job to look. It was also her punishment because she knew that she was responsible for what lay ahead.

"Found them." Steiner's voice came over the radio. For no reason, it garbled again. Then it straightened out.

"Your team didn't get very far." Rykoff sat close. Dr. Kay closed her eyes. The image of Rykoff's mutilated, scared face burned in her mind. She felt his eyes burning through her closed lids.

Looking down, Dr. Kay answered. "They didn't have self-contained breathing gear. Ask your team how they feel."

"They feel fine, Dr. Waterstone. Look at the screen. You know you want to look."

Dr. Kay looked up at the monitor, saw the equipment fallen in the ice and the yellow suited bodies of what had once been her own team. They were lying in contorted positions, a reflection of how painfully they had died. She remembered how quickly it had happened. Their screams haunted her nightmares.

"Bag them and bring them in," Rykoff gave the order into his mic.

"Copy, Dugout."

The hand-held image was jerky as it moved over the bodies. It zoomed in on a bell-shaped yellow hood with a broad face-shield. Underneath, a heavy, black face respirator was still in place. The filter system covered the occupant's nose and mouth. The eye pieces were stained on the inside by a powdery yellow substance. Light reflected back from the glass of the eye pieces. The eyes themselves could not be seen.

"Dugout, this is Batter." Steiner's voice came into Dr. Kay's headset. "I'm going to give you a look."

"Tell him no!" Dr. Kay said to Rykoff. "Tell him to wait until he gets them in isolation."

Rykoff ignored her. He watched the screen.

Steiner made eye contact with the camera lens, then crouched over the dead body and reached for the face apparatus. The camera followed Steiner's gloved hand, as it ripped away the black plastic goggles and air filter.

Steiner's scream seemed to go on forever. It mixed with radio static in Dr. Kay's headphones.

Chapter Sixteen

It was four a.m., when H.I. Tech finished the last file on the computer disk.

The hum from the twin turbofan engines was almost soothing, but no way could he sleep. For restless minds, sleep is not an option. Same thing with a mind that's close to pissing-in-its-pants scared. H.I. Tech was definitely that scared.

He closed the laptop and checked the GPS-linked flight-path display on the fore and aft cabin monitors. The G5's position was over the eastern tip of Puerto Rico. Its air speed was five hundred knots, heading almost due south.

Across the aisle, Doc was well into his second pot of black coffee. Under a beam from the ceiling reading lamp, he was bent over his laptop. H.I. took a long look at him, and words came out all by themselves.

"Just this once, why didn't you just say no?"

Doc didn't answer him. H.I. told himself that was bullshit. "Want to know something, Doc? Dr. Kay should have said no too. The two of you are damn selfish."

"Stop complaining and start thinking." Doc swiveled in his chair, stretched his six-foot-two-inch frame. He pointed toward the back of the cabin.

He followed Doc's stare. In the back of the cabin, April lay slumped in a reclined chair, head turned toward the window, blonde hair splayed all over her blanket. He couldn't tell if she was asleep. He hoped she was out cold. He didn't want her to hear what he was going to say next.

"What did you tell April?"

"Just that her mother was involved in research for the government and that there'd been a problem."

"That's bullshit. She let you get away with that?"

"I didn't give her a choice." Doc took off his reading glasses and wiped the lenses with a pocket handkerchief. "You've had time with the files. What do you think?"

Ever since H.I. had been a little boy, Doc had liked bouncing his ideas off of him, always counting on him, even daring him, to disagree. A good argument made him think more analytically, sort of like Sherlock Holmes and Dr. Watson. H.I. was pretty sure it wasn't much fun for Watson either. He looked at Doc and shrugged.

"Damn thing is amazing, isn't it?" Doc ran a hand through gray hair badly in need of a barber.

"You want amazing?" H.I. felt his temper rising and let it burn through the roof. "I'll tell you what's amazing. Girls are amazing. April Waterstone is amazing. My grades are amazing, given the time I'm not at school. But what I just studied is not amazing. This is seriously screwing with nature, Doc."

"I'm not raising you to take the safe route. Anyone can do the safe route. Extraordinary people, the ones who make the big strides…"

"Take the big chances. I've heard it."

"Taking chances? No! That's gambling. The people I'm talking about take finely controlled risks." Doc's southern accent became more pronounced, slowing his speech and filling his words with a warmth that was not usual for him. He smiled.

"Right, I forgot." H.I. said it with as much sarcasm as he could muster. Doc ignored it.

"I want to know what you think, starting with the Bell Tower object."

H.I. took his time forming an answer. It wasn't that he believed or did not believe in UFOs. In his view probably most people wished at least one of the UFO reports jammed into the human interest segment of the evening news would turn out to be a bona fide, extraterrestrial spaceship. That would be cool and amazing. But he also was sure of the really good reasons why cool and amazing would not happen.

His first conclusion was that those analyzing the data were unreliable. The UFO field was crowded with opportunists making a living off of public fascination. These guys flashed fake or exaggerated credentials. They claimed to be scientists, engineers, or intelligence operatives. They claimed to have inside information on captured spaceships or alien corpses held at secret government bases. But as if to tell himself "let's face it", H.I. realized these guys were nothing more than snake oil salesmen working the media for a buck. And did they ever work the media! Talk about massive numbers of books, news clips, and junk science documentaries. The public had an appetite for it, and the media gladly obliged appetites. After all business was business. But somewhere

among those appearing in front of cameras were decent people who were truly perplexed, even upset by experiences they could not explain. Of more concern, there were within that group a growing number of those claiming to have been abducted by and experimented upon by aliens. But none of them had ever produced even a scintilla of physical evidence. No matter, the undaunted public was still ready to embrace them. Worse, there were mental health professionals willing to magnify the craziness of those who believed they'd been abducted.

H.I. wasn't calling them crazies to be cruel. He even kind of felt sorry for them. Not so for their shrinks. That was the scam part, their psychiatrists. "If you're troubled, it's because you have a repressed memory of an alien abduction."

Talk about violating the first principle of medical care! Do no harm?

A shrink who's taken the Hippocratic oath telling some patient that he's disturbed because he was kidnapped by an alien. A shrink taking money for that kind of garbage and appearing on talk-show television with the poor patients who probably needed some real care. What a carnival side show!

But the UFO field was no stranger to carnival side shows. Anyone could get into that act. Even practical jokesters, the kind of guys who mowed patterns in crop fields and spread the rumors that the patterns implied a visit by alien spacemen. Oh, yeah, right! Sophisticated alien civilizations go around carving patterns in crops. Right!

But not to be misunderstood, H.I. knew for a fact that real scientists had researched UFOs and extraterrestrial life. But the real scientists didn't look squeaky clean either. They

didn't look squeaky clean and they didn't look scientific. They were biased, either for or against. And a real scientist cannot afford to be biased. Doc's rule was that a real scientist must be an objective collector of data and a seeker of the truth. He must admit it when he's wrong and never one-hundred-percent believe it when he is right. But the legitimately credentialed scientists in the UFO field did not follow those rules. Yet somewhere in this mess there truly were those few objective scientists, but they had very little support and even less money. And even then the data collection was less than reliable. And that led to H.I.'s second conclusion: most of the data collection surrounding UFOs was just plain worthless.

For sure, there were unexplained things being seen and reported by normal, honest people. But because these normal people were taking their reports to the opportunists, the crazies, and the biased, any hope of their data remaining clean was lost. And worse, these normal people had to know they would get all kinds of unwanted public attention, even ridicule. So where else could they go? How about to the government? That was the worst option and the crux of H.I.'s third conclusion.

The government was the wild card in the whole field of UFOs. Probably a lot of unexplained stuff observed by normal people was a lot of stuff the government wanted to keep hidden. They would rather have John Q. Citizen believe he saw a UFO than know he caught site of a high-altitude spy balloon, an experimental aircraft, or aviation accidents like jettisoned fuel tanks and unintended missile releases. Not that H.I. thought the government was uninterested in UFOs. Once upon a time, the government had UFO investigations with cool names like Project Sign,

Project Grudge, and Project Bluebook, all supposedly shut down for lack of evidence.

Supposedly! That was the key word.

After the whole enchilada had been shut down, the government's lead investigator, Dr. Alan Hyneck, had gone on to make a death bed confession. His confession was still accessible. It was an admission that he'd released only those investigations concluding with natural explanations. The rest, all of them unexplained by the natural, he'd helped bury. People on both sides of the fence had respect for Hyneck. His last statement bothered H.I. There was, after all, no reason for Hyneck to tell a lie on his death bed.

"We're not playing with a full deck," H.I. told Doc.

"You think that information was withheld?"

"I know it was. The seams are obvious."

"I agree," Doc said.

"Gee! There's a first."

Doc ignored the sarcasm, reclined in his swivel chair. "Assume there are good reasons information was withheld."

"Tell that to Raymond Marsden."

"Agreed again." Doc opened a file on his own laptop and found a satellite photo taken of Alpha Bell Tower within an hour of its impact. The photo was grainy and black-and-white. Alpha Bell Tower was at the bottom of a wedge-shaped crater. H.I. looked at it a long time, a silver half-sphere hugging the ground like a building-sized drop of mercury.

H.I. told Doc what he thought.

Possibility number one: Marsden's object was a sporadic asteroid. But, no way! Asteroids did not light up spectroscopes with tails of hydrogen ions. Nor did they impact the Earth at shallow angles. Nor did they survive impact and maintain a perfect geometric form. Anything with a molecular substance dense enough to survive those forces would be so dense it would sink by its shear weight to the center of the Earth.

Possibility number two: the thing was a comet. Again, no way! Comets could in fact impact the Earth with great destructive force. But like even the biggest of snowballs, they did melt. And they did not leave behind a solid core.

Possibility number three: the thing was an entirely new astronomic phenomenon, some sort of solid core comet. It had a random orbit that slammed it into the Earth at 150,000 miles per hour, and the shock waves killed everything in its vicinity. But, again, no way! The solid object sitting in the Amazon crater was the size of a small warehouse. The energy and force would have been tremendous. A simple equation spelled it out. It was the same equation that would be solving the homework problem Phil Bagley had assigned his math class only hours before. H.I. rubbed the fatigue from his eyes. Had that really only been hours before? H.I. realized he needed sleep badly. He forced himself to concentrate.

energy = ½ (mass x velocity squared)

Pick any mass that you want for RM 1999. At 150,000 miles per hour, you're already up to a multiplier of 32.5 billion before you even get to the mass. If RM 1999 is solid and the size of a building, and if you multiply its mass times 32.5 billion and divide by two, you've got the energy of millions of nuclear bombs. The object itself should have been completely destroyed. The explosion should have sent earthquakes around the globe and brought on the equivalent of nuclear winter, the same as the asteroid that destroyed the dinosaurs. Because said destruction did not occur, said object must have made a soft landing. That led directly to possibility number four: the object was of artificial design.

RM 1999, aka Object Alpha Bell Tower, was capable of its own propulsion and flight. It was either a satellite, a probe, or a spaceship. Its origin could not be Earth. No human technology could decelerate an object from 150,000 miles per hour to zero in such a brief time. The g-forces would squash human occupants into grease and disintegrate any craft of human design. Its origin had to be extraterrestrial.

"My vote is also for number four." Doc said. "But you left out a sub-possibility."

H.I. felt the hairs on the back of his neck rise. "What possibility?"

"That the object is a weapon! A sort of Trojan horse!"

H.I.'s imagination went to bad places. "What sneaks out of the horse after dark?"

"That's the question, isn't it?" Doc went back to his laptop.

H.I. moved to the swivel chair across the aisle from April. He looked at her for a long time, couldn't help it.

"I'm not asleep, Tech." She turned her head. Her eyes were red and wet.

"How long have you been listening?"

"Long enough." She rubbed her eyes. "What in the name of God has Mom gotten into? What's waiting for us?"

H.I. didn't have an answer for that part, or maybe he was afraid of the answer. "About your mom, I think she's okay. I think that's why someone tried to grab you." He stopped talking when he saw fresh tears.

"H.I.," she said. "I know you care about her."

About you too, he wanted to say. But it wasn't the time. Too many other things would have to be said for her to believe it. He watched her turn her head away and fall asleep. He turned out his reading lamp and looked out the window. The sky was an endless field of brilliant stars. Below them, the ocean shimmered in silver. Nothing seemed real.

Somewhere in the upper Amazon jungle, a building-sized object lay waiting in the bottom of a crater. That object was of extraterrestrial origin. And if the rules of physics held true, that object had powers beyond the capability of anything envisioned by humankind. Was it a visitor? Perhaps it was, but if so, it was not a benign visitor. All Earth life in its immediate vicinity was dead. And someone very dear to H.I. had vanished trying to find out why.

H.I. Tech told himself that all he cared about in the whole world was the other someone who had fallen asleep in the chair across the aisle. And if possible he was going to try to get her to some place safe. Like it or not, Doc's comparison of Alpha Bell Tower and the Trojan horse still burned in his brain. So did the question he'd posed to Doc .

"If Bell Tower is a Trojan horse, what sneaks out after dark?"

Chapter Seventeen

The first red body bag slid onto the autopsy table in the isolation lab.

Secure in the safe lab module, Dr. Kay watched through the window of one-inch glass fit into a rectangular hatch separating her from Node 2. Inside Node 2, the hazmat suits were racked. Beyond them, Node 2's far rectangular hatch was also fitted with a large glass window, and through it she could see into the isolation module, where bulky figures in lime-green vapro-proof suits and hoods moved about connected to air hoses suspended from overhead tracks. The figures hovered about the autopsy table.

Dr. Kay glanced upward. The overhead pressure LED confirmed that Node 2 and isolation were negatively pressurized and cooled to 35 degrees fahrenheit. In the event of a breech, the air would move into and not out of isolation. There might even be a small amount of time to seal the breech and prevent whatever killed her first team from getting out.

She checked the integrity of the isolation compartments on her desktop computer. All environmental functions were in the green, pressurized to one atmosphere and cooled with a self-contained system. Monitoring the barriers was easy. Ultra-sensitive pressure and temperature monitors were infrared based, able to detect any leak in the air-tight doors, bulkheads, air ducts, or electrical and communications conduits. The barriers were intact.

Dr. Kay spun again toward the hatch. Her reflection looked back at her. Black hair, dark complexion, and blue eyes. The eyes were tired and frightened, more so than she remembered.

"Are you ready to begin, Dr. Waterstone?"

Rykoff's formless face was suddenly reflected next to hers. His eyes gleamed like violet acetylene torches. She refused to turn and look at him. "Where's my daughter?" she asked.

"En route, Dr. Waterstone."

"I want to know she's okay."

"First you'll do your work." Rykoff looked over her shoulder, across Node 2, and into isolation. Two compartments away, a technician in a hazmat suit turned and moved to the hatch. The overhead air hose followed, moving on a track and interfacing with a metal pass-through in his back. He hand-signaled Rykoff.

"Now we will see what got Herr Doctor Steiner's attention." Rykoff clicked on the intercom and a monitor fed from a camera near the autopsy table. Rykoff keyed his mic. "Steiner, we have a time schedule."

"Ja, ja. This is no little green man from Mars." Steiner was visible on the monitor, leaning against steel cabinets and keeping his distance from the red body bag. Like the others, he had shed his aluminized over-cover outside the decontamination chamber and was working in a lime-green hazmat. Beyond his face plate, his eyes swam behind thick spectacles.

"Herr Doctor Steiner is afraid, isn't he." Rykoff's voice was laced with sarcasm.

"Anyone would..."

"But Steiner is not," Rykoff answered, "anyone."

Rykoff seemed to wait for Dr. Kay to contradict him. She didn't. He continued. "Fifteen years ago, Steiner was in Leipzig. A pathologist. Autopsied human beings murdered in every conceivable way. Imagine it, and Steiner has seen it."

Dr. Kay listened. She'd never liked pathologists. Too dark with their humor.

"In his younger days, Steiner liked this kind of work." Rykoff whispered, his breathing touching Dr. Kay's throat. She didn't like having Rykoff stand that close to her. It made her blood cold. He laughed. "Did you know that he trafficked in organs?"

She cringed but tried not to show it. Rykoff leaned in again to whisper, this time touching her ear with what was left of his mouth. "Herr Doctor Steiner was caught in the act. The Russians, the GRU, knew that when they recruited him. They didn't care. They recruited him to work at Sverdlovsk. Bio-warfare stuff. Botulina and Anthrax. Bad stuff! Steiner wasn't afraid then. So why is he afraid now?"

"Guess we'll know soon." Dr. Kay closed her eyes, tightened every muscle in her body, and waited for Rykoff to move away. He didn't. She forced her eyes toward the monitor.

Inside the lab she could see Steiner's assistants unzip the red bag and remove the body. A second camera rolled into position on an overhead track, and its lens zoomed in on the autopsy table. Dr. Kay changed feeds on her monitor, filled her screen with the dead man's yellow body suit and black face respirator. She recognized that he wore level C protective gear only, not fully encapsulated but open at the ankles and wrists and neck. No self-contained air. Just a filter breather. Dr. Kay made herself look, told herself it was her punishment to see the death she had caused.

Rykoff used the keyboard to focus the lens on the dead man's face, buried in a respirator. The eye pieces were layered in a yellow film. Rykoff activated a video recorder. On screen, a gloved hand reached for the head gear. Dr. Kay held her breath, told herself she wouldn't be able to look at the face of someone she had worked with, eaten with, joked with. Not the face of someone she'd killed.

"We'll see if this one is the same as the other." Steiner spoke into his microphone and looked into another camera lens. Beyond his face plate, his spectacles were fogged. He was hyperventilating. "You will need a strong stomach for this, Ja."

Dr. Kay tensed again. She felt her stomach roll into a knot. There had been four team members, all alive a week ago. Which face would she see first?

Steiner removed the face respirator, and the dead man's face came off with it, leaving eyes swollen the size of golf balls, weeping a sticky, silver-yellow film. The face came apart in Steiner's hands, its layers of skin, muscle, and connective tissue all blackened, deeply blistered and layered in a pale chalky substance.

Dr. Kay felt the floor rising toward her. She crouched and held her head between her knees, tasted the throat moisture that comes right before throwing up. Rykoff pulled her upright.

Steiner's voice trembled on the intercom. "I'm seeing massive soft tissue necrosis of the head. Skin, fascia, and mucous membranes are all sloughing apart in my hands." Steiner moved his trembling, gloved hands to unzip the dead man's level C protective suit. "The same lesions extend down the trunk and the extremities. Entry site for our hot agent is skin and respiratory and mucous membranes, Ja?"

"Impossible!" Dr. Kay shook her head. Hot agent was a bio-warfare designation for a microbe that could cause disease or death in humans. Every microbe had a specific portal of entry into humans. The portal could be ingestion, membranes of the genital or urinary tract, broken skin, the respiratory tract, or direct blood entry. No organism could do all. She shook her head again. "Not possible."

"I can only state what I see, Frau Doctor." Steiner answered. "I've never seen anything like it."

Dr. Kay recovered. "I want to see histology."

"Copy that." Steiner answered. "We'll make frozen sections and start the permanents."

Steiner collected tissue samples, froze them in liquid nitrogen, shaved them to single cell layers, and stained them. Within ten minutes the frozen sections were under microscopes linked to the video network. "Transmitting now."

"Copy that." Dr. Kay watched the microscopic images fill the monitors. She identified the separate preparations.

"I'm seeing peripheral blood, skin, connective tissue, and muscle."

The skin specimen showed epidermis sheared away from underlying fat and coagulated from lack of oxygen. Only shadowy remnants of the fat remained, all of it broken down into gelatinous fluid.

"You ever see this before?" Dr. Kay keyed her mic.

"Ja." Steiner answered. "The enzymes of certain Streptococcus. The flesh-eating bacteria, as your media calls it. But not on this massive a scale."

Dr. Kay rotated the image to the next slide. Muscle cells were ravaged, their tissue architecture obscured by a shapeless, granular substance. Steiner had added common basophilic stain that turned the granular substance blue. Blue permeated the muscle on a massive scale. Surrounding the substance was very little white cell infiltrate. The body's defenses had been overwhelmed much faster than they could mount an inflammatory response. Watching, Dr. Kay felt sweat form. Nothing killed as fast as what she was seeing. Nothing!

Steiner centered the microscopic field on the blue substance. "What is your guess, Frau Doctor?

"Liquefaction necrosis." Dr. Kay answered. She referred to cell death massive enough to reduce solid tissues to liquid residue. "But I've never seen it on this level. It's like something tried to digest this man alive."

"Agreed." Steiner replied.

"Elaborate, Dr. Waterstone." Rykoff interrupted.

"You see this in two circumstances in people," she told Rykoff. "One is flesh-eating bacteria. The other is pancreatitis. You know about the first. As for the second, when your pancreas goes, it leaks its enzymes into your belly and they eat every fat tissue they touch. Eat right through your tissue planes, break your fat down, and bind the garbage to calcium. Leaves goo that looks like chalk."

"On this level?" Rykoff asked.

"Never."

"Find the microbe that did this."

"This could not have been a microbe." Dr. Kay used a remote control to rotate the microscope lenses to high power and oil emersion. There were no bacteria in the microscopic field. She told Rykoff.

"Try other stains," he answered. "This has to be the work of a microbe."

"Something very mean, Ja." Steiner's voice crackled over the intercom.

Dr. Kay ordered Steiner to prepare alternate stains in the permanent sections. She used her remote control again, rotating a new slide under the microscope lens. The new slide was a smear of the dead man's blood. The microscopic field was filled with ruptured red cells. "Massive hemolysis," she said. "That means…"

"I know what it means." Rykoff interrupted. "Burst blood cells, like what is seen in snake venoms."

"But not on this level." She closed her eyelids, rubbed them. "Not bursting nearly one-hundred percent of the cells in a peripheral smear. Not on this level. Hemolysis is usually slow and survivable. This destruction is total."

On screen, Steiner opened the dead man's abdomen from pubis to sternum with a knife, then nervously returned the instrument to a sharp's well. One of his assistants opened the chest with a saw.

Steiner's voice trembled again. "Lungs are filled with blood and fluid. Liver is mush. Massive third spacing in the abdomen."

Dr. Kay nodded. The process implied a rapid collapse in the integrity of blood vessel walls. The blood vessels had literally wept their fluid contents into the lungs, liver, and abdominal cavity, yet another lethal process distinct from the previous two.

On screen, Steiner opened the skull. The brain was intact. Whatever had occurred had not crossed the blood-brain barrier. That meant the man had likely been fully conscious while he was dying. Dr. Kay did not need the autopsy results to make her aware of that fact. She'd heard all of the screams on the radio. The pain must have been terrible.

"What could have done this?" Dr. Kay rubbed her eyes.

"A microbe, Doctor Waterstone." Rykoff moved to the glass window and looked across Node 2 and into isolation. "An extraterrestrial microbe."

"Can't be."

"You don't except the existence of extraterrestrial microbes."

"I do accept it." She'd seen the evidence. First the amino acids, the basic building blocks of proteins, found in a carbonaceous meteorite that fell in Kentucky. Amino acids were the building blocks of proteins. And proteins were among the building blocks of bacterial walls, enzymes, and intracellular organelles. So the find of amino acids from space made it possible. Then there had been the Martian meteorite found in Antarctica. Maybe it contained microscopic fossils, little indentations where there had once been living bacteria that were not of the Earth. "I do accept it," she said a second time. "But not here. There are no micro-organisms in the field."

"None that can be detected with your one stain, and perhaps none that can be detected by light microscopy. Perhaps there is something smaller, something that electron microscopy might show. Perhaps we are dealing with a virus."

"A virus doesn't make sense," Dr. Kay answered. "It has to be something that can carry on its own life functions." She told herself bacteria made sense. Bacteria were self-sufficient in a variety of environments. Bacteria had cell walls or membranes for protection, had microscopic organelles to burn energy and build proteins, had a nucleus to house genes. So even an extra-terrestrial bacteria of non-carbon origin could sustain its life on Earth. Bacteria were very self-sufficient.

But not so a virus.

A virus was just a strand of gene wrapped in protein. It lived by attaching its gene to a complimentary site in an animal or plant gene. Then it hijacked its target, took over the plant's or animal's machinery, and ran things toward its own end. Reproduction and invasion. A virus could not live outside of its target.

The thing from the crater could not be a virus.

Not unless it was made of RNA or DNA, just like the genes of every form of life on Earth. And even then, the predator couldn't be a virus. Because no single gene strand could be basic enough to lock on to a site in the genes of every form of life on Earth. Not even Earth viruses could do that—jump multiple species or jump from animals to plants. Attack every life form in their path? Impossible!

"It can't be a virus. A virus is too target specific." She said it again. She started to argue her point, but stopped. She realized it would be a good thing, Rykoff's moving in the wrong direction. A good thing!

"Do the electron microscopy anyway," Rykoff said. "Look for something small."

"You hear that Steiner?" Dr. Kay spoke into the intercom. "We're going to work in teams." She waited for Steiner to acknowledge, then turned to Rykoff. "Team A does the micro work. Team B does toxicology. Let's see if we can ID some form of poison."

Rykoff nodded.

"This is going to take some time," she told him.

"You have very little time, Dr. Waterstone." Rykoff answered. "You have until the outside construction is complete to isolate and identify the virus. That gives you thirty-six hours."

"That can't be done! The cultures alone will take days, if they grow at all."

"I hope you're wrong, Doctor." Rykoff studied her, hungry eyes taking in all of her. His face was flaccid as a rubber mask, cold and dead. "If you fail, we inoculate test subjects and see if we produce the disease. Once construction is complete, we'll have over a hundred Jivanos. Excellent test subjects, I think. " Rykoff turned toward the hatch to Node 1. He spoke without looking back at her. "Use your time well." He exited, closing the hatch behind him.

Dr. Kay looked at the clock. It was one a.m. She cursed. "It can't be done."

The cultures would be useless. Whatever substance or substances poisoned and digested her coworkers inside their suits would destroy any culture media she had. And electron microscopy would show no alien virus. The predator couldn't be a virus. She cursed Rykoff harder, and then the realization hit her.

Rykoff understood she would fail. He didn't intend for her to succeed, only intended to keep her busy until the Jivanos were ready. He intended to inoculate them, use them to isolate the hot agent. He'd make her work with him. And she would do what she was told because he had April.

"What is the protocol, Herr Doctor Waterstone?" Steiner's voice came over the speaker.

Dr. Kay felt the sweat form under her arms and down her back. She tried to think.

"The protocol, please." Steiner's voice was louder.

She punched the intercom and gave orders. "Team A inoculates the cultures. Aerobic and anaerobic media plus cell cultures."

"What conditions?"

Dr. Kay thought about duplicating conditions in the crater and gave instructions. "Drop the incubator temperature. Increase the CO_2 concentration." She made guesses on both but told herself it didn't matter. All of the culture media would denature or die. She paced the floor, thought hard, and clicked the intercom again. "Team A also preps the electron microscope. Use the necropsy specimens."

Steiner acknowledged her orders and asked about team B. Dr. Kay told him she'd have instructions for them shortly. She switched off the intercom and paced and thought. If she could ID a toxic agent, Rykoff might reconsider his plans for the Jivanos. An ID of a toxic agent would not give

Rykoff the weapon he sought. He'd have a beginning for further study, and that would be all. She'd buy time. Maybe!

Steiner called her again on the intercom. "Your orders for Team B, Frau Doctor?"

She played her intuition and hoped that the toxin was a protein. Proteins were built of amino acids, and she had the machinery to ID amino acids. Her software could determine the relative concentrations of various amino acids and use them to determine the identity and relative concentrations of specific proteins. It could be done. Dr. Kay gave Steiner her orders, took a seat next to a monitor, and wrapped herself in a blanket. She waited.

The monitor screen relayed a feed from the isolation lab. Dr. Kay watched one of Steiner's technicians in a hazmat suit inject a large sample of one of her dead coworker's body fluid into a centrifuge, where it mixed in solution with a biochemical detergent. If she was correct, if the toxin was a protein, the detergent would render it soluble.

It was two a.m. when Steiner stood in front of the camera and showed her a tray of over twenty test tubes of washed solution made from the body fluids. The liquid in each tube was turbid. Dr. Kay downed coffee, nodded, and ordered the next steps to be run in parallel.

Steiner approached the first analyzer machine. The machine wasn't much to see, just a big box, a very sophisticated box that was compact, self-contained, automated, and computer driven. She watched Steiner inject the tubes of turbid fluid into an entry port and sensed the fluid passing internally into a horizontal column of cellulose. Bottles fitted atop the boxy machine drained buffer solutions into the apparatus where it mixed with the solutions prepared from the dead men. She pictured them mixing and diffusing through the cellulose, each diffusing at a different speed, each speed determined by chemical structure. They were purified in the cellulose, separated into individual proteins, fast ones and faster ones. Slow ones and slower ones. Each pure protein fed into the ultraviolet chamber at its turn. Each got bombed with ultraviolet light and recorded a spike on a graph. Each batch of distinct protein fed into a separate tube held in a rotating barrel tray.

Science by machine, Dr. Kay told herself. High Pressure Liquid Column Chromatography (HPLC), one of the weapons of the modern warrior. She was the modern warrior. A pale scientist in a lab coat. She watched the machine record spikes on paper and feed the paper out of a slot.

HPLC SPIKES
TUBE NUMBER   1 2 3 4 5 6 7 8

Dr. Kay tried to count each tube as it filled in the spinning barrel. She lost count at fifty. She suspected the number would go to two hundred tubes, two hundred substances. Each would have to be analyzed. There wasn't time. She stopped watching, poured another cup of coffee, and let it sit. It was foul and syrupy. She wrapped her blanket tighter and fought the urge to sleep.

At four a.m. Steiner examined the culture dishes and confirmed Dr. Kay's fears. The culture media was denatured, destroyed. So were the cell cultures. There would be no growth. She told him to continue the toxin ID. The toxin had killed the culture media. It was still active.

She slumped in her chair and cursed Rykoff, reminded herself that he was insane. She fell asleep pondering whether the insane ever really slept, wondering if Rykoff slept. She went to sleep hoping she could escape for a while. She was wrong.

The dream floated Rykoff's face close to hers. His battered flesh and bones opened for her, and deep within him she saw a damaged trachea unable to remain open during sleep. He told her he needed a machine to sleep. She was with him as he fit the black plastic mask to his face, fit it tight enough to pressurize his collapsing trachea and keep it open. The mask and the machine allowed a monster with a crushed face another night of sleep and another day of life. She was with him because he forced her, controlled her. So she waited, thinking and planning the unimaginable. Waiting for him to sleep so she could pull the mask. But her hands wouldn't obey. They wouldn't kill. .

A voice woke her from sleep, a German voice magnified across an intercom. "Dr. Waterstone, electron microscopy is ready." The voice belonged to Steiner. He was excited. "Rykoff was correct."

Rubbing her eyes, Dr. Kay sat at a keyboard and switched feeds on her monitor. The screen filled with the grainy black-and-white image transmitted from the electron microscope in the isolation area. The electron microscope wasn't really a scope at all. The things it sought were too small to be seen directly, so it created shadows of them using electrons like an X-ray machine used gamma rays. It made cross-sectional shadows of the smallest living structures in existence. The process was simple. Specimens were shaved down to a single cell layer and dried, then coated with a thin layer of gold to make them conduct electrons. The coated specimens were placed inside a vacuum chamber and bombed

with electrons. The electrons passed through the specimen and painted shadows on a charged plate, just like an
old-fashioned, grainy, black-and-white photo, producing a
photo of the human cell and everything inside.

"Rykoff was correct," Steiner said a second time. He was
giddy. "We have our virus."

She didn't look at the images immediately. She closed
her eyes, pictured the living cell, knew the architecture like
any room in her house. In her mind, her vision swept across
the cell nucleus, the control center of the cell, then moved
into the cytoplasm and counted the organelles. They were
as familiar as furniture in a room. The tubular mitochondria, the mighty mitochondria, were microscopic factories
that burned fuels to drive life. Drifting beyond them were
more tubules, the endoplasmic reticulum, where proteins
were manufactured and packaged. All of the proteins
were then wrapped in spherical beads called Golgi bodies, ready for transport across the cytoplasm. She marveled
at the cell's being a complete machine containing all the
organelles needed to carry on life.

"Did you not hear, Frau Doctor?" We have the virus,
Ja."

She opened her eyes and looked at the grainy images of
skin and muscle cells. The cytoplasm of all of the cells was
swollen with tiny spheres. Swollen to bursting point. She
made herself wake up, told herself that maybe Rykoff was
right. Maybe the little spheres inside the human cells were
viruses, using the cell's machinery to replicate themselves
until the cell burst. She looked a long time. Then the truth
hit her. She keyed the intercom.

"No. It's not viral particles. Looks like it, but it isn't."

"But Frau Doctor, it's…"

You're seeing Golgi bodies, Steiner." Golgi bodies, spherical packages of protein produced by the cell itself. Not a virus. Just cell protein production.

"Can't be Golgi bodies, Herr Doctor Waterstone. The cytoplasm is packed with them. No cell produces Golgi at that rate."

"Unless something is driving them to. Maybe it's a response to whatever killed them."

"Can't be right. They died too quickly."

"Dr. Waterstone, we have mass spec," a technician called her on another channel. She changed her monitor feed, saw the boxy mass spectroscopy machine in the lab. This one was also self-contained and automated. Micro-samples of the body fluid solution were injected into the machine and bombed with a beam of charged particles, breaking the body fluids down into smaller molecules and then into ionized elements. Gas moved the ions into an electric field. Different ions landed at different places on a plate, and knowing which elements landed where on the plate allowed a computer to do the identification.

Dr. Kay stared at the computer screen, looking at the pattern of dots that represented the different elements in the solution. She blinked and stared a second time. There was carbon, lots of carbon. Then there was hydrogen, nitrogen, oxygen, and sulfa.

"Whatever did the damage, it's carbon-based and made of protein." The technician said.

"Copy that," Dr. Kay whispered. Like Earth life! Carbon-based! She gave orders. "Run the proteins we ID'd against earth-knowns. See if we have a match in the software. Maybe even a close match in weight and composition."

"We have over three hundred tubes from the HPLC." Steiner said. "Which ones do we run?"

Dr. Kay rubbed her eyes and fought off sleep. She tried to think. The answer would be the largest quantity of purified protein. Those would be the ones that spiked in a tight cluster. She looked at the graph and gave the order, then watched the work on her monitor.

Another box in another corner of the lab. An amino acid analyzer.

Steiner selected the appropriate tubes and ran them. The process was simple. Run each specimen through an electrified gel. Each amino acid settles in one place according to its structure. Match your results against substances already known on Earth. Let the software match your unknowns and give you the answer.

Dr. Kay fell asleep again. It was six a.m. when Steiner woke her. Her eyes and face hurt, made it painful to shake off sleep and see in the overhead lights. She staggered to the intercom.

"We have it," Steiner shouted. "Our mysterious little bastard is not so mysterious, Ja."

She looked at the results twice, told herself she was hallucinating, maybe having a nightmare. She looked a third time. "This can't be!" She called the service module. "Tell Rykoff to get down here now."

Rykoff did not come to her compartment. Under armed guard, she was taken to him in the service module. He was drinking black coffee and eating breakfast that had been mushed in a blender. She faced Rykoff and pulled up her data on his network computer screen.

```
NEUROTOXINS.....................Present
HEMOLYSINS........................Present
NUCLEOTIDASES..................Present
HYLARONIDASES.................Present
PROTEOLYITIC ENZYMES......Present
```

(quant to follow)

Dr. Kay explained. "There is no one toxin. There are dozens." She swallowed and looked him in the eye. "They peak the same as organic toxins from dozens of known species of poisonous snakes and spiders from our planet, peak the same as known Earth bacterial exotoxins and endotoxins and enzymes that eat soft tissue. They even peak with organic plant poisons. This thing is a biologic impossibility. It will kill anything in its path. Anything."

"I want the extraterrestrial microbe that produced those toxins."

"I didn't say extraterrestrial. I said toxins. More specifically, I mean Earth toxins."

Dr. Kay started to remake her point, but stopped abruptly when she saw the new data displayed. Her software had run the quantitative analysis, extrapolated a total body concentration of the toxins. She could not believe what she was seeing, but she knew the calculations were probably correct.

"This is not the work of a microbe, Rykoff. Do you understand that?"

She tried to swallow, but had no saliva. "The man on the autopsy table had over two liters of toxins, two damn liters. This thing is a nightmare!" She almost stuttered. "Whatever did this, it poisoned those men and tried to digest them inside their suits, every part of them except their brains. It did the same to every plant and animal across a mile radius. It even killed bacteria. No microbe can kill like that." She stopped talking, tried to fight the images in her brain. Something big and alive, hidden in the carbon dioxide fog. She forced the thought from her mind and looked at Rykoff.

In the light from the monitor bank, Rykoff's eyes were brilliant violet. Their gaze was frozen on her face. Rykoff was listening to every word, thinking hard. It scared her, what he might be thinking.

She continued. "There's something behind this that is intelligent, that can think and plan. Something more destructive than…"

"You are wrong, Doctor." Rykoff's eyes darted, then focused. "This is a virus."

"No virus can do this."

"No virus from Earth." Rykoff laughed. "Can you imagine the sheer potential for terror? Terror is the most important element of any weapon."

"You're not listening to me. This is not something you can control."

"Of course I can control it. You'll help me." Rykoff moved his face to within an inch of hers. The closeness made her nauseated. "You have the amino acid sequence of the toxins, and you have a lovely gene sequencer in the lab. That means you can build a DNA probe. You can use the probe to survey the bodies and find the virus."

"That won't happen. The technology is not that fast. Won't happen in thirty-six hours. Not in thirty-six months."

"You are stalling, Dr. Waterstone."

"No, I'm not! Whatever did this, you won't find it in the bodies. All you'll find is the toxins, not the thing that put them there."

"Then we will have to go to the source, won't we?"

Rykoff looked at the infrared monitor. The Alpha Bell Tower object was a motionless orb of yellow in the gray cold. It was waiting.

Chapter Eighteen

H.I. was asleep over the laptop, and he was dreaming. But it felt real. A cold sweaty kind of real. Marsden was warning him. But his warning was far away, then gone. H.I. fell through blackness. There was nothing to grab and no way to stop. Whole worlds were falling, and somewhere far away, almost beyond vision itself, were dim stars. He fell through interstellar space, through constant night. Somewhere close, he felt a dreadful presence.

The silver object wasn't falling. It was feeding on cosmic particles, fusing them in its belly and using the energy to propel itself faster and faster. Within it there was life and intelligence. H.I. understood its purpose and felt terror.

And then the falling stopped.

The vastness was a blackboard, where chalk and erasers moved frantically, propelled by frightened hands. The voices were fast and barely comprehensible, the world's greatest scientists confronted by something beyond their comprehension. One asked for Marsden. But Marsden wasn't present. The arguing got louder. The same word was uttered over and over, in hushed tones.

"Extinction!"

They sensed the object hurtling through endless night. H.I. did more than sense it. He followed it across a journey not measurable by human time, a distance of 32600 light years. Its beginning was in the nuclear bulge of the giant spiral galaxy later to be called the Milky Way. Its destination was a solitary, outer-reach star that lay between two far spiral arms of the galaxy. The third planet of that star was green and teeming with life.

The journey reached its end sixty-four and a half million years before humankind.

The writing on the blackboard became more furious. The shouting rose. The voices lost all reason. They filled with terror. The conclusions were undeniable. The data from the fossil digging proved what they all feared. The end of life was not gradual. It was sweeping and sudden.

"Extinction."

The Earth spun in the blackness below. The object smashed into Earth's atmosphere, hurling wind storms in all directions. It soft-landed in a primordial swamp, under the eyes of a herd of massive beasts feeding on plant life. Their tiny brains didn't register the object's presence. But inside the object, something intelligent watched them feed and knew it was seeing a dead end that could not progress beyond the primitive life forms who had ruled the planet for 175 million years. It knew their simple, unreasoning brains could never develop intelligence and tools. It knew their continued existence meant that no smaller life-form could evolve either.

"Extinction!"

A scientist wrote the word on the blackboard. A dozen other hands did the same. Marsden was suddenly with them, warning them. "The end came from outer space."

H.I. watched the beasts he recognized as dinosaurs die. Their tiny brains remained intact, their eyes open and aware, even as something horrible ate the flesh from their great skeletons and sank their remains into the muck. Only the smaller animals survived. The smaller animals lived to scrounge and feed on what little flesh remained from the great beasts who had once hunted them. They began to give birth. Their brood was different.

They were evolving.

H.I. sat facing the blackboard and the scientists who clustered around Marsden. He felt the presence of someone seated next to him, but he knew better than to look. The scientists parted, and Marsden turned from the board. His face and body were smashed and bloody. He raised a hand that hung at an odd angle, bone protruding through skin. He pointed past H.I., and slowly H.I. turned in the direction Marsden was pointing. H.I. caught a flash. It was a flash of red hair and green eyes. Malone!

Then the warning came from Marsden. It echoed in his brain as Malone and the classroom disintegrated into constant night and dim stars. H.I. fell through a cold, black void, and as he fell he heard Marsden's warning over and over.

The object was back. After sixty-million years, it was back.

H.I. felt hands touching him. He expected them to feel like broken bone and crushed flesh. Instead they were soft and tapered. He heard a voice calling him, but it wasn't Marsden's. It was a soft voice, one he wanted to hear for the rest of his life.

"Tech! Wake up. Please wake up." April was shaking him.

H.I. tried to force his eyes open. They hurt. His heart was pounding in his chest, and he was sweating. His stomach was in his throat. He felt himself falling. At first he thought he was still dreaming. He wasn't.

"Tech! Wake up. Something's happening."

Daylight streamed in through aircraft portals and across April's soft face. Beyond her, hazy daylight diffused through dense gray clouds. She looked scared. He realized why immediately. The turbofan jets were high pitched, almost whining. They were descending fast.

"Where are we?" he asked.

"You tell me," she said nervously.

The GPS-fed display on the fore and aft monitors had traced their flight south across Venezuela and over the Guyana highlands. The plane icon was interposed somewhere near the upper Amazon basin, over the Rio Negro River. The destination indicator settled just inside Brazil, a small green circle captioned with "Villa Lobos."

April blurted again. "We're going down."

H.I. didn't get the chance to answer. They hit an air pocket. The plane dropped like a stone. A hundred feet below and a few seconds later, it recaptured its lift and stabilized. April retched. She had nothing to throw up. H.I. put his arm across her shoulders and held her.

"I'm okay." She turned her face away. H.I. guessed she didn't want him to see her sick. "Thank you," she whispered as she cleaned her face. "I hate heights."

Doc wasn't in the cabin. H.I. left April strapped in her seat and groped his way forward using the tops of seats. In the cockpit, he found Doc bent over Malone and Ramsey and trying to tell them how to fly the plane. Typical Doc.

H.I. looked over Malone's and Ramsey's heads. Dense gray clouds and rain drops slammed the glass. No visibility. In the right seat, Ramsey pressed his headset to his ears, addressed Malone and not Doc. "Tower's real nervous. He wants us to divert."

As if on cue, the plane bounced hard.

"No shit, he wants us to divert." In the left seat, Malone had both feet locked on the rudder pedals and both hands gripped to the yoke. Her eyes were glued to her flight instruments, all displayed graphically on CRT. Rain pelted the window harder. Still no visibility, but she was descending.

"Where's your horizon?" Doc asked.

"Somewhere between this soup and the ground." Malone answered calmly. "Feeling lucky this morning?"

Ramsey interrupted. "Tower wants an answer."

"Tell them we're diverting to Manaus." Malone said.

"We don't have the time." Doc interrupted.

H.I. could tell Malone was really pissed. She took her time answering Doc. "Let me fill you in about the landing field at Villa Lobos. Picture a rotten little wooden shack with an old radio and a beacon. The field isn't really even a field. It's just a high, dirt road that serves small aircraft—when they clear it." Malone adjusted her throttles to compensate for another air pocket. She gave the turbofans more power. "This decision is my call, and I don't feel like killing myself this morning."

"Then don't. Use your glass cockpit properly, make your approach into the wind, and land this plane at Villa Lobos." Doc turned to H.I. "Get back to your seat and buckle up." He moved back to the cabin.

"Is this safe?" H.I. asked.

"No," Malone answered.

"Feeling dangerous, Malone?" Ramsey lifted an ear-phone from one side of his head and grinned. H.I. couldn't tell if he was worried.

"Nah," Malone answered. "Dangerous is landing on the deck in a storm in the Med. That could ruin your day. That's dangerous. This is stupid."

"He's right about the time, Malone."

"I know that."

"Shit hot." Ramsey said it without flinching. H.I. knew the expression "shit hot." Carrier pilots used it. They had ice for blood, just like Ramsey.

"Shit hot." Malone muttered back. "Tell the tower to turn on the beacon and get the traffic off the road." She waited for Ramsey to do as she ordered, then gripped the throttles in her right hand. "Pitch her up a little and give me ten degrees of flaps. Watch the glass."

Watch the glass meant watch the fancy displays on the CRT screens. H.I. knew all about glass cockpits, how they relied on satellite feeds and how they could locate an aircraft within six feet of its actual global position. He also knew they could not make up for bad weather and a short, muddy runway.

"Stupid," was the last thing H.I. heard Malone mutter. He moved to the cabin, took the seat next to April's and tightened his belt. Doc sat directly forward, his six-foot-two-inch frame jammed into a swivel chair. He was read-ing documents, indifferent to what was happening, as if he not only expected but demanded that it turn out okay. H.I. saw that April was beginning to look sick. The turbulence threw her into H.I. a second time. H.I. caught her and held her head. Then he saw something bad outside of the window.

Liquid was spraying out of the right wing. H.I. knew it was fuel. Malone was dumping fuel. A bad sign! She anticipated a hard landing and didn't want a fire. H.I. tried to keep April's head positioned so she wouldn't see what Malone was doing. But she pushed her way out of his grip.

"Let go, Tech! I mean it."

She didn't finish. In that same second, Malone extended the flaps. The plane bled off air speed and began rolling its wings side to side as it hovered just above stall speed. April pulled her belt gut tight, and started praying. H.I. interrupted.

"Pray for good math."

"What?"

"There's good math and bad math. Pray for good math." H.I. explained that good math was a big number for the runway and a small number from braking distance. Anything else was bad math.

"You're crazy. You know that?" She squeezed a pillow against her chest and kept praying.

Beyond the window, the clouds broke into wisps smothering a rain-soaked green canopy maybe a hundred feet below. The wings rolled again, as the landing gear rumbled into position. Malone compensated with her throttles. The engines whined louder, and the fuselage shook. The plane felt mushy, as if there were lots of play in Malone's controls. H.I. knew what Malone was trying to do, make her approach at just above stalling speed and drop the two-engine jet on the dirt road that served as a runway.

"It's a fact that the back of the plane can survive a crash." H.I. shot his mouth off without thinking.

"Shut up, Tech!" Her eyes narrowed into blue storms. "God!"

The math hit H.I. The runway was a section of dirt road built on a ridge in the rain forest. How long could it be, a thousand feet or two thousand feet? How much of it was dry this time of year? Probably enough for a light, single engine aircraft with a landing speed of say fifty knots. The G5 they were flying was probably ten tons of aircraft landing at 150 knots. That was ten tons traveling at four-hundred-and-twenty-five feet per second. That could eat two thousand feet of runway in a little over four seconds.

Bad math! Very bad math! H.I. began doing some praying of his own.

"Tech, you believe in God?" April looked at him.

"Big time," he answered.

Malone stalled out the G5 at the edge of the runway. She dropped it like a rock onto the soft earth and stood on her brakes. In the muddy ground, they didn't do any good. There just wasn't enough friction. She retracted the flaps to let the jet sink its weight into the ground. That didn't help, either.

The trees rushed by the windows at a hundred miles per hour.

Malone extended the reverse thrust vanes on the engines. The sudden g-force threw H.I. into his belt. His head slammed the seat. Engine thrust howled into the vanes and over the wings. The vibrations shook the fuselage. It felt like the jet hit a wall.

The trees rushing by began to slow as the jet settled into the mud and bled off speed. Ten tons of G5 stopped just short of the runway's end and the rotting shack that served as a tower. Wash from the engines pelted the hand-painted sign that read "Villa Lobos Airoporte."

Malone killed the engines. She took her time coming back to the cabin. Doc took off his reading glasses, folded up his documents, and looked out of his window. He spoke to Malone without looking at her. "Looks like you did it on about three thousand feet of runway. I counted on the head wind. I was right."

Malone leveled angry green eyes at Doc. He ignored her and diverted his attention to Ramsey, who opened the forward door and dropped the steel stairs. Air rushed into the cabin, air that was almost too hot and wet to breathe. Impenetrable rain forest hugged the ridge on both sides. Between the trees, it was dark. It felt alive.

"Where's your contact?" Doc asked Malone.

"We call them assets," Malone answered. "He's coming. Meanwhile we wait."

April cradled her head in her hands between her knees. Blonde hair splayed everywhere. H.I. applied a cold rag to her neck, and she muttered thanks. He realized she'd said thanks a lot on the flight. Maybe that was progress. Maybe she'd even begin talking to him again. He told himself they'd have lots of time to work things out. Because wherever Doc and Malone and Ramsey were going, he wasn't going to be with them. And neither was April. H.I.'d see to it.

Twenty minutes later, an open jeep pulled up beside the jet. In the passenger seat a local official in a sweat-stained uniform lit a cigarette while starring at the jet and shaking his head. From behind the wheel a tall, balding Gringo emerged wearing a filthy polo shirt and jeans that clung to his wasted body. The Gringo's face was chinless and narrow, divided unevenly by a thin nose. Behind aviator shades, his eyes were still visible. They were beady enough to remind H.I of a rat. And like a rat, the Gringo found a dark place to perch. His was in the shadow between the cockpit and the cabin. The Gringo seemed to like it there.

"I'm Briggs, with State." Gringo's accent was thick, Bostonian. He avoided eye contact. "Are you Malone?"

"That's right." Malone sized him up, didn't seem to like what she saw.

"I'll need your passports," Briggs said.

Malone handed them over to Briggs who handed them to the sweating official who'd entered the plane behind him. Briggs rattled off instructions in Portuguese. The accent didn't sound right. Maybe he'd learned in Boston. A lot of Portuguese lived in Boston. It didn't matter about the accent, though. The local official seemed to understand as he thumbed through the passports.

"I was told you might need my help," Briggs said.

"No help. We just need transportation."

"We need it *now*, Mr. Briggs," Doc interrupted. He looked at Briggs like he would a bug. Watching, H.I. got a bad feeling.

"Sure thing, Sport," Briggs collected the passports back from the local and put them in his own pockets. "It's your tour."

H.I. helped April out of her seat, and she almost smiled at him. It was a weak smile, but a smile for sure. More progress he told himself. He grabbed up his duffel and Doc's, then remembered that one of the duffels held the laptops and the discs. The dream came back, and he shuddered before forcing himself to shrug. Alpha Bell Tower wasn't his problem. And dreams were bullshit, just a mind exercising its connections as receptors restored themselves during sleep. H.I. watched April and began working on their escape. He began feeling sure of himself, very sure.

Chapter Nineteen

Malone took a last look at the G5. Its wheels were settling in the mud of a road that was little wider than a donkey path and carved out of a ridge in the rain forest. She took Doc's word about the road's length, 3000 feet. Way too short for a runway, she knew. Ramsey had to know it too.

"No way I made that landing, Ramsey."

"Don't kid yourself, Malone. You're a damn good pilot."

"That's right. I'm a pilot. Not a magician!" She muttered under her breath what she'd never say out loud, that she'd witnessed a miracle. She didn't believe in miracles. She turned away from the jet and the road.

Briggs led the way to his jeep. Doc, Malone, and April followed. H.I. hung back with Briggs's Brazilian official as he watched Ramsey try to secure the landing gear of the jet. The official had something H.I. needed.

The official's eyes seemed to be locked on the landing gear. Supporting ten tons of aircraft, the landing gear were sinking in the wet earth. There wasn't much for Ramsey to do, just lock things up. The official was probably wondering how Ramsey and Malone were going to fly out. If H.I. could have spoken Portuguese, he could have told him that Ramsey and Malone weren't going to fly the jet out at all. There was no way they were going to get the gear out of the mud. And even if they could, there just wasn't enough runway for take off. If H.I. could have spoken Portuguese, he could have told him that millions of U.S. tax dollars worth of jet was going to have to be disassembled on the ground and trucked out. But it wouldn't matter. The official wouldn't give a damn about the tax dollars.

Nor did the official need to know what was going to happen to the plane. He didn't need to know about Malone and Doc's job or know about Alpha Bell Tower. No doubt, Briggs from State hadn't told him the truth, and maybe Briggs didn't know much himself. Either way, the official could just chalk up Malone's landing to another stupid Yankee stunt. Besides, the official was probably more concerned about the fees he was going to extort.

Maybe he deserved to know the truth.

A hundred miles or so away from Villa Lobos, something frightening had come down from the sky. And all around it, there had been death. Maybe knowing what H.I. knew, the official would decide to run like hell and take his neighbors with him. In his place, H.I. would have run. But of course H.I. understood the big picture. He had Doc's Bell Tower discs replaying in his head. His dream was replaying too. Both made running seem sensible. He didn't have to remind himself how much he prayed Dr. Kay was still alive at Crash Site Alpha Bell Tower or that Doc would come back in one piece. Doc's plan – just showing up at Crash Site Alpha Bell Tower as if he were dropping in on a colleague – seemed like bad one. H.I. had another one—one that made sense.

But H.I.'s plan required some things from the bored, sweating official. Those things were still in the official's breast pocket. They were H.I.'s and April's passports. The other passports, Malone's and Doc's and Ramsey's, weren't important. Just his and April's. But it looked like the official was not going to be giving them back any time soon. That was going to make H.I.'s plan tough. Tough but not impossible

H.I. walked to Brigg's jeep and climbed in back between Doc and April. Malone rode shotgun. Briggs drove. As they entered Villa Lobos, H.I. found his expectations met. Nothing but a narrow stretch of river beach and a single, red mud road. Nothing but a few tin-roofed buildings and a stretch of thatched shanties separated the black water of Rio Negros from dense rain forest. One of the tin roofs belonged to the town's only hotel.

April climbed out of the jeep and entered the hotel. H.I. hung back.

Briggs walked Doc and Malone to the river bank, passing a tin-roofed warehouse. The warehouse fronted the first pier, which supported fueling tanks. Briggs led them along the beach, stepping around Indian dugouts and approaching a boathouse on the far side. The boathouse led to a second pier. Briggs took Doc and Malone around the house and out of sight. H.I. turned to Briggs's jeep.

It appeared to be the only vehicle in town. That was a good thing, but H.I. would have to confirm it. The tank was full, and Briggs's keys dangled from the ignition. Two more good things. He looked in the direction of the river and waited. Doc and the others were still out of sight. He crossed the street and edged along the boathouse until he could hear their conversation.

The pier was creaking under their weight. It was that damn old. Built of native hardwoods, H.I. guessed. The hardwoods had probably been taken from the high rain forest, and decades of rainy seasons had probably taken their toll. The pier looked bad, but the transportation Briggs had arranged looked worse. Doc was okay about it. Malone wasn't.

"They'll hear that loud piece of shit in fricking Rio De Janeiro."

"No one will pay her any attention." Briggs threw his cigarette stub into the black water.

Malone gave Briggs's boat a second look. Her expression remained unchanged. The boat rode low in the water. Her forty-foot hull supported one flat deck covered by a six-foot roof. In the stern, her twin gasoline engines were mounted in an open hold shared by fuel drums. The wheel and throttles were configured inside a wooden house aft of the bow deck. Her name was *Portos Blanco*, White Dolphin. No doubt about it, *Portos Blanco* looked like she had been around a very long time. Briggs meant her to be the transport all the way to Crash Site Alpha Bell Tower. And Doc meant to go.

Briggs seemed nervous. "When she isn't chartered, she runs supplies downriver. Next run is in the morning."

"We want to leave now." Doc took off his jacket and tried to ignore the heat. He was still wearing his roll neck. It was drenched. He had to be sweltering.

"Next river run is in the morning, sport. Engine needs a spare part."

"I don't think you heard my associate." Malone tried to keep her temper even. She didn't succeed.

"I did hear him, Malone. Port engine needs a new ignition solenoid. I've done all I can."

"Do better."

"This isn't Brasilia, Malone. And I'm not the station chief." Briggs fumbled with another cigarette. "In case you haven't noticed, this place is kind of primitive. I was sent here six months ago, and I was told to keep my eyes open. But nobody told me what I was supposed to watch for. Nobody told me shit, Malone, until I got a satellite call from you. So lay off! I'm doing the best I can."

Doc cut Malone off before she had the chance to answer. "We'll be ready at first light, Mr. Briggs."

Doc left Malone standing alone with Briggs, threw his jacket over his shoulder, and carried his laptop toward where H.I. was standing. H.I. moved as fast as he could to the street-side of the boathouse and flattened against a wall. He heard Malone catch up with Doc. They stopped walking. Malone was angry.

"Let's get something straight, Doc! You stick to your job, and I'll stick to mine."

"While you're sticking to your job, check out your asset. Something's not right about Briggs from State!"

"Like I said, that's my job."

"Your job is also to get us downriver and in the backdoor at Crash Site Alpha Bell Tower. Get us a chance to look things over first and go in second. We agreed about that, Malone."

"I haven't forgotten."

"Then don't screw it up by making a lot of noise up here."

Bad plan, Doc! It was all H.I. could think. Bad plan! He crossed the street and made it back to Briggs's jeep. He turned as Doc and Malone came into view behind him. They were both sweating in the heat. She was standing almost under his face. Alone in front of the boathouse, they were visible to every set of eyes on the single street that was Villa Lobos. Indian eyes, mostly. Maybe a few laborers. The Indians probably thought them to be tourists. Maybe the tourists were tired and quarreling after a long journey. That was common. They would be better after a night's rest.

Briggs was nowhere in sight. Doc and Malone talked for a while, but H.I. couldn't make out what they were saying. Then Doc walked toward the hotel. He almost looked worried. Only almost! As far as H.I. knew, Doc was never a worrier. As Doc walked toward the hotel, his eyes were fixed on it and not on H.I. Having read about Villa Lobos on one of the discs, H.I. thought he knew what Doc was thinking.

Thirty years earlier, an entrepreneur loaded with American capital had built the hotel to serve as headquarters for a company that was going to mine manganese from the Amazon basin. The entrepreneur and his company were long gone. His three-story, wooden hotel had stayed open for business. Open for American Yuppies with enough money to take exotic vacations and tell themselves they were on an adventure. Personally, H.I. Tech would have used the same bucks to go Cancun. But that was just him wanting an ordinary life and all of that. As for the hotel in Villa Lobos, its tourist days had ended with Alpha Bell Tower's drop from the sky. They'd ended courtesy of the local government and the CIA.

H.I. distanced himself from Doc and climbed to the hotel verandah. Doc continued making mental notes. H.I.

thought Doc was probably noticing that the hotel domi-
nated the street, was built high above the river bank, and
backed up directly against a canopy of the giant soft wood
trees. The front was good. It was secure. A second-floor balcony commanded the beach, the river, and the thatched
shanties stretching away in two directions. It faced the only
other big structures in sight—the warehouse and the town's
water tower. The front was good. The back wasn't good at
all. In back the verandah and the second-floor balcony
touched the rain forest. The back was impossible to secure.

And judging by what had happened already, security
had to be big on Doc's list. H.I. knew Doc didn't give a
damn that the hotel walls were covered in green tiles, which
in rain held up better than paint. He did care that from
the hotel verandah and its high, European windows, the
narrow white beach of the Rio Blancos was visible. So were
the native dugouts, and so was Briggs's jeep. And so was the
boathouse and the *Portos Blanco*. The hotel occupied a strategic position that also rendered it accessible from every
direction and impossible to defend.

Doc finished studying Villa Lobos and headed straight
for the verandah. H.I. held his breath as Doc neared the
jeep. The keys were still in the ignition. The tank was full.
And the muddy road under the wheels led right back to
civilization. Anyone could borrow it, even Doc's sixteen
year old son who was now thinking more clearly than Doc.
H.I. watched Doc pass the jeep without looking. Careless of
Doc. Good for H.I.

April still wouldn't want to escape with him. But maybe
he wouldn't give her a choice. Maybe he'd tell her that the
two of them were just going for a short drive. He wouldn't
tell her that the drive was as far from Briggs and Malone

and Ramsey as the gas and the road would take them. He thought about that road and April. He tried to forget the other things.

But forgetting was not the order of the day. The dream he'd had on the plane was still with him. So was the classified stuff he'd seen in the discs. So was Object Alpha Bell Tower. He told himself that remembering would give him incentive to follow his personal plan. But he didn't need incentive. The dream tied things together in one ugly word that wouldn't leave his head. *Extinction*!

"Where's Ramsey?" Doc stopped on the verandah. He was sweating in the heat.

"Securing the plane."

Doc nodded and started into the hotel. H.I. stopped him. He couldn't think of any other way to do it. So he just blurted things out and waited for Doc to laugh. But Doc didn't laugh.

"You dreamed Bell Tower was here 65 million years ago, changed the pattern of evolution on Earth, and killed the dinosaurs? It was Bell Tower not an asteroid that did the deed?"

"That's most of it."

"And the more you think about it, the more it bothers you?"

"Pretty much."

Doc looked damn serious. But serious wasn't what H.I. wanted to see. Doc answered thoughtfully. "That stuff about the asteroid and the dinosaurs is just a theory."

"I feel better hearing you say that." H.I. felt himself relax, but he was premature.

"Actually, it has merit."

"What has merit, the dream or the theory?"

"Maybe both. There is data."

"The good kind of data or the maybe kind of data?"

"Depends on who you believe." Doc said all of the experts agreed that the dinosaurs died in one event. He brought up stuff H.I. already knew including the K-T boundary. The K-T boundary was a geologic line observed consistently throughout the world. Underneath it, dinosaur fossils existed. Above it, they didn't. The K-T boundary was loaded with iridium. And iridium came from asteroids.

"Which sort of does prove that they died from an asteroid, not Bell Tower." H.I. felt better for a second.

"Doesn't necessarily prove anything," Doc said. "Some think a volcanic eruption did the dirty deed, killed the dinosaurs with a nuclear winter and spread Earth core iridium over the planet surface. And the volcano theory is completely plausible."

"But a volcano doesn't explain the Yucatan crater." H.I. referred to the crater supposedly made by the asteroid that ended the dinosaurs. Satellites could still see it on infrared beneath the Earth's surface. A crater 150 miles in diameter where the big one came down! Doc disagreed.

"It may not even be a crater. And it may not have been caused by an asteroid. Any asteroid impact big enough to make a crater that big should have broken fragments off the continental shelves and moved them across the K-T boundary. There's no evidence to that effect."

"Unless that something made kind of a soft landing." H.I. didn't like hearing his own words. They took him back to the dream, a huge object hovering over a primordial swamp and dinosaurs dying with their flesh consumed.

"Science is a work in progress," Doc answered flippantly. "I taught you that."

Doc headed for the hotel door, stopped, and turned. "The same scientific school that believes in the asteroid theory also links six major fossil-documented episodes of evolution with geologic evidence of asteroids. Evolution and cosmic events. Makes you think about it."

"I don't want to think about it."

Doc left the verandah. H.I. didn't. The breeze carried the damp smell of the rain forest floor. He looked down the red-dirt slope to the river bank and to the black water of the Rio Negro. He knew why the water was black. Decomposing life forms from the floor of the rain forest washed into its bottom, and their humic acids made it black as outer space. The water teemed with life, brilliant, colored aquarium fish of more variety than anywhere else in the world. Scientists could not explain why. More holes in science. H.I. didn't like it.

A hundred yards away from him, Malone stepped onto the beach. Briggs stood at her back. They both studied the river. H.I. figured Malone was planning the route to Crash Site Alpha Bell Tower. H.I. knew the geography from the discs. The Rio Negro flowed south fifty miles through a valley bordered by thousand-foot highlands. At the end of that valley, it swung east into another valley and grew in width. Five-hundred-fifty miles away, in Manaus, it formed the massive Amazon itself. At the end of the first valley, the Rio Negro was joined from the west by a tributary that descended from pure, uninhabited rain forest.

Somewhere in that rain forest, Alpha Bell Tower was waiting in the bottom of a mile-long, wedge-shaped impact crater. He didn't like thinking about it.

Malone looked once in H.I.'s direction and then back toward Briggs. They began arguing. H.I. rooted for Malone. After all, she had saved his life twice. He appreciated that favor, even though he knew it had not been personal. Rooting for Briggs was out of the question. H.I. watched them for a long time. Then he entered the hotel.

Doc was leaning against a desk at the base of hand-carved stairs and standing next to an old Indian, dressed in shorts and a tattered T-shirt. Doc looked preoccupied, didn't seem to notice the Indian. H.I. did notice.

The Indian had skin like weathered brown leather and hair as black as the Rio Negro. His legs bore scars. From piranha, H.I. surmised. But what caught his attention were the round objects the size of oranges dangling from a pole the Indian held over his shoulder. H.I. knew what the objects were and kept his distance.

The Indian turned in his direction, stared with eyes as cloudy as glass, and smiled without teeth. His tattered shirt read *Mort's Deli, Green Street, N.Y.* Maybe a tourist had bartered with him, exchanged the shirt for something native. How many pure Indians were left in Brazil? Fifty thousand? They were vanishing from disease and starvation as their rain forest was taken away from them by outside interests while the government looked the other way. The thought drove H.I.s dream back into his head. He remembered the one word on a blackboard, scribbled by nervous hands. Extinction!

He took a second to look at the objects dangling from the Indian's pole, turned away, and entered the cantina. The floor was cracked linoleum, clean but old. There were tables and chairs, the folding kind he'd see in a school cafeteria. April was asleep at a far table, collapsed as if she'd passed out. Her face was nestled in blonde hair. H.I. sat next to her and watched for a while.

She was beautiful asleep. She was breathing softly. He knew she wasn't having nightmares. Her face was relaxed and motionless. Her eyelids were as smooth as flower petals. She was definitely not having a dream. His impulse was to let her stay asleep and sit there with her. But there were things he had to tell her.

He didn't notice that the old Indian had followed him. H.I. leaned his face close to hers, swept the blonde hair from April's ear, and whispered. She woke up to the round objects the old Indian suddenly dangled between them.

"Oh, my God." Her eyes went wide. Her face was inches from the round objects. She lost all of her color. "Get them away from me!"

H.I. sent the old Indian away, handed April a bottle of water, and watched her take big gulps. She was still shaken. "Were those what I think they were?"

"Shrunken heads," he answered, "but no one you know."

"Shut up, Tech."

"It's cool. Certain tribes of the Orinoco and Amazon…"

"I don't want to hear."

"Sure you do. These guys take the heads of their enemies and remove all the bones through the nose without touching the scalp or face. Then they…"

"I told you I don't want to hear about it." She put her hands over her eyes. "For God's sake, get a life."

"I do have a life." Over April's shoulder, H.I. watched Malone join Doc at the desk, then turned to April and made a major mistake. "We're getting out of here, you and me."

She didn't answer, just stared at him and looked a little shocked. Maybe there was even a little venom in her eyes. Exactly the reaction he'd anticipated. Things were going to be tough. After a second, she pulled at the sweater she'd borrowed from Malone and changed the subject. Her message was clear. "Does it get cold here at night?"

"I doubt it," he shrugged, "Are you hot in those clothes?"

"What do you think?"

"Why don't you lose the sweater?"

"I don't have anything under it." She shifted her eyes to the old Indian and then turned back. Her eyes were blue storms. "How much do you want for that Timex you're wearing?"

The watch was a digital day-glow mounted in black plastic. H.I. told her she could have it.

"No way are you giving it to me. I owe you what, thirty bucks?"

H.I. nodded. She looked in the direction of the old Indian and took the watch. She said nothing, just stuffed it into her pocket. She forced an innocent smile as Doc approached the table.

"Your rooms are next to ours." Doc said. "Get some rest."

Malone came up behind Doc, eyed April then H.I. "Lock your doors. And don't open them for anyone except for us."

Chapter Twenty

There was no night or day in the habitat module. There was only the constant cold and the one longitudinal corridor that accessed a train of windowless, steel compartments. Dr. Kay slept fitfully in her compartment. She felt the dread even in dreamless sleep, waking over and over to the infrared image on the desktop monitor only inches from her face. On screen, the half-sphere gave off a yellow heat signature surrounded in cold gray. The sphere was motionless.

It was waiting.

She shifted her gaze to the time display. It was 1400 hours when she heard the mechanism unlock the pressure-sealed compartment door. She sat on the edge of her cot as the door hissed open. A mercenary stood in the subdued light from the corridor. Like Bulldog, he was twice Dr. Kay's size, and he wore a sidearm. His smell, sweat and cordite, stung her nostrils. He spoke with a heavy, Russian accent.

"To go to service module. Rykoff!"

She swung her long, bare legs out of the cot, too exhausted to care that the mercenary was watching her. He continued watching as she turned her back to him and dressed. The fatigues Rykoff had given her were filthy. They were too large on her slender body. She did the best she could to tuck things in while from the corner of her eye she caught sight of the alarm blinking on the monitor. She ignored the mercenary, punched the keyboard, and pulled up the source display.

DECONTAMINATION ACTIVE
BIOCIDE SHOWER
PHASE 1 CIDEX
PHASE 2 VESPHINE
PHASE 3 DET

Team one was decontaminating, she told herself. They were using chemical jets. She found the jets themselves by opening a file to the internal security cameras. She selected the feed from the decontamination module, where the isolation lab and the tunnel interfaced. On screen, the jets were at high pressure, spraying team one. The chemicals pelted the bulky figures in lime-green hazmat suits, washed over face plates, and reflected rainbows.

No good, she told herself. Chemical decontamination might do no good at all. Not against an extraterrestrial unknown. Not against whatever had come from Alpha Bell Tower. And she promised herself that whatever the unknown was, it was not a microbe.

No microbe could jump all species and kill all life in its path. And that was what something from Bell Tower had done, killed all Earth life in its path.

She locked her eyes on the screen. The first chemical jets sprayed concentrated glutaraldehyde. It would instantly destroy cellular proteins. The second jets sprayed phenol, a highly toxic industrial poison that would tear apart cell walls, kill cell proteins and inactivate cell enzymes. The third jets sprayed a concentrated detergent meant to denature proteins and make them slippery. The detergent was supposed to make any foreign substance slip off of the suits. All in all, the jets would be very useful against Earth microbes in operating rooms and labs. But what came from Alpha Bell Tower was not of Earth origin.

She imagined herself shouting it in Rykoff's twisted face. "You're wrong, Rykoff. This is nothing you can control. This is a biologic nightmare."

"Service Module." At her back, the mercenary raised his voice. "Rykoff!"

Dr. Kay nodded, sat back, and slipped into boots that were too large. She avoided the mercenary's stare and fumbled with the laces. Her mind raced.

How much good would isolation do if somehow Rykoff were right, if the massive killing was the work of a space microbe? Maybe no good at all. She remembered that a year earlier, Jennings had attacked the problem of space microbes at the first NASA workshop on astrobiology. She'd watched Jennings go through his slides.

NASA STRATEGIC PLAN
ASTROBIOLOGY
DEFINITION: THE STUDY OF THE LIVING UNIVERSE, PROVIDING A SCIENTIC FOUNDATION FOR THE MULTIDISCIPLINARY INVESTIGATION OF THE ORIGIN AND DISTRIBUTION OF LIFE.
PART ONE: WHAT WE KNOW—LIFE AT THE EXTREMES

She remembered Jennings's munching on candy bars as he'd lectured. Earth microbes were damn hardy, much hardier than anyone thought. They'd been found living in volcanoes, living in temperatures beyond boiling. They been found living in strong acids inside caves and living at pressures of twelve hundred atmospheres at the bottom of the Marianas Trench. They'd even been found living in outer space because they'd hitched a ride on satellites and somehow survived the temperatures and vacuum and cosmic radiation. Earth microbes could also withstand time. They could live in a dormant state. One strain had survived forty million years inside the gut of a fossilized bee. The prehistoric strain had been liberated in a lab and subsequently grown in culture.

"If Earth microbes can be called hardy," Jennings had hit his last point between bites of chocolate, "we'd expect space microbes to be damn near indestructible."

Indestructible! The word echoed in Dr. Kay's head.

She finished tying her boots and stood. The mercenary slipped a callused hand to the holster of his sidearm and nodded toward the open door. In the same breath, he smiled at her. She cringed and turned to the monitor.

UV DECONTAMINATION
DESSICATION MODE
TEAM 2 IS ACTIVE

On screen, the men in the hazmat suits were stepping under ultraviolet lights. The ultraviolet radiation was supposed to break down cell DNA. Maybe effective. Maybe not. Dr. Kay switched the camera feed to Node 2, where a second team led by Steiner was climbing into rear entry suits. Their large hoods were resting on their shoulders.

She watched them a long time and promised herself she would find some way to make them fail, some way to make them destroy themselves in the process.

"Go now!" The mercenary gave Dr. Kay a shove away from the monitor and into the corridor. She stumbled and caught her balance. She walked ahead of him.

They walked the length of the habitat module and stepped through double hatches into Node 1. They took a ninety-degree turn through another set of double hatches and into the service module. Rykoff was waiting at the central computer station, the back of his head to Dr. Kay as she was shoved forward.

"Are you rested, Dr. Waterstone?" Rykoff spoke without turning. His voice was soothing, almost hypnotic.

"Does it matter?"

"Of course it matters. I don't want any mistakes."

"Then the answer is no. I'm not rested."

She watched Rykoff's ears tighten as he turned toward her. Beneath his eyes, his hideous face was dead. Seeing him, her reaction was disgust, then fear.

"Dear, Doctor Waterstone." His eyes gleamed violet. "I can't have any mistakes due to fatigue. Nor can I fall behind schedule." He punched the remote keyboard he held in his lap.

At Rykoff's back, the monitor switched camera feeds. A wide-angle lens was focused down a narrow clearing that stretched thousands of feet into the distance. The sides of the clearing were lined by the scorched stumps and wreckage of what had once been a rain forest. Alpha Bell Tower's final approach, Dr. Kay reminded herself. She watched the screen, as tractors moved in and out of view. What was being built was not clear to her. She watched as armed guards bullied Jivanos Indians into view. The Jivanos were moving in threes and carrying long rolls of heavy, synthetic material.

"What do you see, Dr. Waterstone?"

"Men with guns," she answered. "And slaves."

"Slaves for now. Test subjects later." Rykoff's voice filled with sympathy, almost regret. "If you are unable to lead my team directly into the object, my alternate protocol is human inoculation and microbe isolation." His voice drifted. "A sad necessity. Science makes us live with sad necessities. For you, it would be like Africa."

She started to tell Rykoff that no one had died in Africa. But her guilt stopped her.

"We both live with our pain, don't we?" Rykoff's eyes bore into her. "I imagine your father wanted so much for you to see the world his way. I imagine his sadness and pain the day you learned how the world really works."

"How does the world really work?" She felt the sarcasm in her voice. She fought to control her temper. Losing it would do her no good.

"Science is driven by war and commerce," Rykoff spoke. "Science for the sake of knowledge, your father's science, rides somewhere in the backseat. I imagine your father's pain when you climbed in the front with the rest of us."

I am not one of you, you bastard! She wanted to say it, wanted to spit it in Rykoff's face. Instead she tightened every muscle in her slender frame. She reminded herself that Rykoff was a psychopath.

"Where's my daughter?" Dr. Kay changed the subject. "You told me I'd see my daughter."

"Your daughter is in Villa Lobos."

Dr. Kay saw it in Rykoff's eyes. He was telling the truth. She heard her own voice answer him, knew she was also telling the truth. She stammered as she spoke. "Keep her there. Keep her away from this and I'll do what you want."

"You're too tired to do what I want."

"No! I just need some coffee and some food."

"You're tired, Dr. Waterstone." Rykoff sounded regretful. "Go back to your quarters. Rest and dine while I order Team Two to stand down. After you've rested, you can run my alternate plan. Your daughter will be here by then, and the first Jivanos test subjects will be ready."

"That won't be necessary," Dr. Kay forced strength into her legs. She stood tall and looked directly into Rykoff's face, hiding her revulsion. "I will direct your team into Bell Tower. I will find your microbe." She controlled every muscle in her face. "I want to."

"You want to?"

"Yes." Her mind raced to find a way out. There was none, or she was too exhausted to think of one. She controlled her voice, convinced herself she was saying something she believed. "You're right about me. You're right about the microbe."

Rykoff studied her face. She kept her voice strong, told the truth as she now believed it. "I want to do this. I will do this. Just keep April in Villa Lobos."

She looked away from him and fixed on the screens, where Steiner's team was suited and ready. She glanced at the infrared. The Bell Tower object was motionless and waiting.

"Take the co-command mic, Dr. Waterstone." Rykoff pointed. "We have a schedule to keep."

Chapter Twenty-one

H.I.'s room was between April's and Doc's. The walls were plaster over wire and wood, with the plaster pealing in a lot of places. Paper thin, he told himself. He knocked and got a hollow echo. Not a good thing for what he had in mind. He knocked again. From her side, April shouted for him to stop. He opened a window, turned on the ceiling fan, lay on the bed, and waited.

April's room got quiet fast. For a while, H.I. could hear Doc moving around in his. Probably Doc had a lot of things on his mind, like asking himself why he'd been cutting Malone so much slack. It wasn't like Doc to let other people have a say in how he did his job. In fact, Doc wasn't being Doc at all, and that bothered H.I. Malone bothered H.I. too. She kind of reminded him of a grade-school crush, the red hair and green eyes, most likely. Of course, the grade-school crush had been his second-grade teacher. And there was a big difference between her and Malone. Malone killed people instead of reading stories to them. And from what H.I.'d seen, Malone enjoyed it.

Malone was supposed to be on their side, he reminded himself. But it was also clear that she wasn't sharing everything she knew. Orders or her own initiative? No way to tell! Ramsey was holding back, too. He struck H.I. as the kind who didn't trust anyone. Probably he was even more dangerous than Malone. All in all, Doc should have been keeping them both on a tight rein. And the Doc he knew would have made sure it was a damn noose, not a rein. But Doc wasn't being himself.

H.I. lay on the bed, stared at the ceiling, and waited. Eventually Doc's room got quiet too. That left nothing to hear but sounds drifting up from the river, birds and occasional voices in Portuguese. The voices mixed with laughter and faded. Maybe the natives were still talking about the tourists. Maybe in the Amazon they had something like a siesta. Either way, with the heat and the stillness, it was easy just to go to sleep. Easy except for the fact that his mind was still racing. He had definite things to do and very little time.

He ticked the minutes in his head, wishing he hadn't given April his watch. He gave himself an estimated twenty minutes before he made his move. Twenty minutes of sleep meant REM time, when dreams made noises from the outside world less likely to disturb the brain. He hoped everyone else in the hotel was into some serious dream time. He got up and moved quickly.

His door was locked on Malone's orders. He put his ear to it and listened. Malone's and Ramsey's rooms were directly across the hall. The flooring was bare and would creak under foot. It was impossible for anyone to move without being heard. He listened and got nothing except the outside noises, something scampering on the tin roof.

Hearing nothing was perfect, if Malone and Ramsey were in their rooms. But it was just as likely that one of them was going to be on watch at all times. H.I. kept that in mind, went to his window, and climbed to the balcony.

The direction he took was away from Doc's room. Better judgment told him to move fast, slip under April's window, and keep moving. But better judgment wasn't in the cards. He stopped even though he knew he was taking a stupid risk. If she was awake and saw him, he'd have either come up with some lame story or tell her what he had in mind. Either would cause a delay, and he couldn't afford a delay. His better judgment was correct, but he didn't care. He stopped and looked.

She was asleep under a sheet, one arm crooked under her head and her face angled toward the window. He watched her wrestle, eyes moving behind closed lids and mouth making little cries. REM time for sure, when rapid eye movements signaled the presence of dreams or nightmares. Eye movements were the same with both. But given what she'd been through, hers had to be a nightmare. He wanted to wake her right then, free her and take her with him. But that would come later.

He followed the balcony all the way around the building to avoid passing Doc's room. The deck was blocked from the sun by massive branches and green moss. He heard howler monkeys, figured they were looking down on the humans without a clue about what they were seeing. Just like the humans who were looking down on Crash Site Alpha Bell Tower at something they could not understand.

The moss padded his steps. He edged under the open windows, counted three and figured they belonged to

Malone, Ramsey, and Briggs. No sounds came from inside. Maybe the three of them weren't in their rooms. That would be a bad thing. He froze at the top of the stairs and studied the street.

Briggs's jeep was still parked in front, empty just like the native dugouts on the beach. There was no one in sight. Maybe because it was the middle of the afternoon and it was too hot. At least, that was the reason H.I. hoped there was no one in sight. He dropped to the first floor, stayed against the wall, and followed the verandah around the back. There were no windows or doors in back. The back of the hotel was where the generator had been positioned. Absent windows and doors meant less noise from the generator's motor and therefore much happier hotel guests. The generator was built inside a shack a dozen paces away from the wall. It sounded like an old lawn mower, but he wasn't interested in the generator. His first target was parked next to it—an old Chevy truck. The old part was good. It made things easy.

There was no lock on the hood. Once upon a time, car manufacturers and buyers weren't so worried about theft. The good old days, maybe. He opened the hood, disconnected the battery and hid it inside the trees. Probably there was another battery somewhere in town, but it would take time to find it. The time part would be important to April and him. He closed the hood on the truck and followed the hotel wall.

It wasn't that he was running out on Doc. Far from it! Doc wasn't thinking straight, and he was. What he was doing was maybe saving Doc's life. Maybe saving Dr. Kay's too. For sure and most important, it was saving April's. As for Dr. Kay, she had to still be alive at Crash Site Alpha Bell Tower.

There was no other explanation for April's attempted kidnapping. Doc seemed to have missed that connection, or maybe he didn't care. Doc wasn't being himself. He'd always told his medical students to group a patient's symptoms under one diagnosis. It seemed to H.I. that was the kind of advice that could be applied to anything. There were no coincidences in life. If two bizarre events were occurring in the same place and at nearly the same time, they were likely related. Doc seemed to have missed that first point. Two thugs had tried to kidnap April at the same time Doc had begun looking into Dr. Kay's loss of contact from a top security site. Both related? Bingo. But Doc had either missed or ignored the connection.

Doc had missed the second point also, the point that April had made herself. Her kidnappers had planned to take her to the airport, and so had Malone. Both parties had wanted her to travel, and maybe both parties had wanted to take her to Dr. Kay. Coincidence? H.I. didn't think so.

Two many bad ideas were in motion. April's going to Dr. Kay, not a good idea! Doc's just dropping in at Crash Site Alpha Bell Tower, not a good idea!

The site was protected by fifty American marines and a contingent of local army. Both were in communication at all times with their respective superiors. And the site was a little over a hundred miles from Villa Lobos, where Briggs was handy with a satellite phone. But supposedly neither Briggs nor military bosses had heard anything. A simple communication problem? No way! And whatever had gone wrong at Bell Tower had gone real wrong. At least part of the real wrong involved a people thing. April's attempted kidnapping proved the people part. And that was something Doc

could not solve. What was he going to drop in and fix that
fifty marines couldn't handle? Hey, folks, you having a problem? Can I help?

Doc wasn't thinking. H.I. was.

He followed the far side of the hotel to the street and
saw Briggs's jeep still parked in front. Across the street he
could see two sides of the far warehouse. Beyond the warehouse a cluster of shanties hugged the street as it snaked
back into the rain forest. There was no way he could get to
the warehouse from the hotel without being in plain sight.
So he stayed inside the trees and followed them to the shanties. Then he doubled back and approached the warehouse
using the river bank. A second truck was parked on the
bank. This one was rusted and resting on wheel rims. Not
a problem. There were only three vehicles in Villa Lobos.
One was junk. One he'd put of commission. And the last
one he'd be borrowing.

The last part of what he had to do was the hard part.

He walked across the street like he had nothing to
hide. He stopped at Briggs's jeep, pretended to admire it,
slipped the keys out of the ignition and into his pocket. He
walked to the hotel slowly, took the stairs to the balcony,
and retraced his steps around the back. He planned what
he was going to tell April. She'd ask a lot of questions.

How far were they going to get? Answer was the American
consulate in Manaus, five hundred miles away. Truth was probably only as far as the road or the first tank of gas would allow.
In all likelihood, "as far" really meant only as far as the next village, where the official who'd met them at the plane had their
passports. The official would have a phone or radio. He'd call
Briggs, and Briggs would tell Malone. Malone would have to

tell Doc. But there'd be no way for them to catch up. Still, H.I. preferred his first thought. Get to Manaus.

Would they be followed? Answer was it would be best if they tried to follow them. Trying to follow them would delay the trip to Alpha Bell Tower. That might just save Doc's life. By the time Doc was on his way, H.I. would be using the official's phone or radio to make two calls. The first would be to the American consulate to tell them what was going on. The second would be to CNN. H.I. figured that CNN had probably reported on the shootings in April's neighborhood and had in turn been fed some kind of cover story. CNN would be salivating over the chance to talk to April. They might even send a helicopter to get the two of them personally. And by that time, things would be would snowballing.

The snowball would roll all the way to Washington. Real help would be on the way by then, not because it was the right thing to do but because there would be some political mileage to be made. In comes the cavalry. Doc is safe. And so is Dr. Kay.

H.I. liked his version of how things were about to work out, but knew it was at best a stretch. Probably it was a lie. Truth was no one would believe him. Truth was that Doc would count on him to keep an eye on April while Doc pressed on to Crash Site Alpha Bell Tower with Malone and Ramsey. April and he would be safe. The others would not.

He slipped passed April's window and climbed back into his room. He parked the keys under his mattress, and opened the door. The floor creaked. He waited for Malone to burst from her room and demand the keys. Her door stayed closed. He knocked on April's.

She answered on the third knock. She came to the door wrapped in her bed sheet. Her eyes were puffy. She rubbed them and looked pissed. "What do want, Tech?"

"See if you're okay." Lame thing to say, he knew.

"You want me to be okay, then leave me alone."

He nodded. She'd hated his guts for a long time. On the road there'd be time to talk and straighten things out. But that would come later. First he had to lie. First he had to tell her that he was supposed to take her in Briggs's jeep to meet the others. He looked at her and made himself believe what he was going to say. But she spoke first.

"Go back to your room, Tech. Get some rest." She started to close her door. He grasped the edge and held it open. She stared back at him and waited for him to let go.

He thought of the two them on the road, talking and at last making up. He thought of the two of them in the official's village making calls to bring the cavalry. But the cavalry would never come. They'd be leaving Doc and Dr. Kay on their own.

"What do you want, Tech?"

"I just thought you might be having bad dreams. I just wanted to see if you're okay."

"I'm okay, Tech. Get some rest."

He took his hand from the door. She didn't close it right away. She looked at him for a long time. Her eyes softened. She slowly closed the door.

He stood there for a while. Even the most complicated problems had the simplest answers. It was never a question of knowing what to do. It was question of choosing. He went back to his room and retrieved Briggs's keys. He planned to return them after dark.

No matter what happened, H.I. Tech was clear on what he was going to do. He was going to go with Doc to Crash Site Alpha Bell Tower. And no matter what happened or what it cost, he was going to protect April Waterstone.

Not the End